LAUGH
TILL
YOU
CRY

Books by Joan Lowery Nixon

The Making of a Writer

Mysteries

A Candidate for Murder
The Dark and Deadly Pool
A Deadly Game of Magic
Don't Scream
The Ghosts of Now
Ghost Town
The Haunting
Murdered, My Sweet
The Name of the Game Was Murder
Nightmare
Nobody's There
The Other Side of Dark
Playing for Keeps
The Séance
Search for the Shadowman
Secret, Silent Screams
Shadowmaker
The Specter
Spirit Seeker
The Stalker
The Trap
The Weekend Was Murder*!*
Whispers from the Dead
Who Are You?

Series

Ellis Island

Land of Hope

The Orphan Train Adventures

Caught in the Act
A Dangerous Promise
A Family Apart
In the Face of Danger
A Place to Belong

Orphan Train Children

David's Search

LAUGH TILL YOU CRY

JOAN LOWERY NIXON

DELACORTE PRESS

Published by
Delacorte Press
an imprint of
Random House Children's Books
a division of Random House, Inc.
New York

Visit us on the Web! www.randomhouse.com/teens
Educators and librarians, for a variety of teaching tools, visit us at www.randomhouse.com/teachers

Library of Congress Cataloging-in-Publication Data

Nixon, Joan Lowery.
Laugh till you cry / Joan Lowery Nixon.
p. cm.
Summary: Thirteen years old and a budding comedian, Cody has little to laugh about after he and his mother move from California to Texas to help his sick grandmother and he finds himself framed by his jealous cousin for calling in bomb threats to their school.
ISBN 0-385-73027-6 (trade)—ISBN 0-385-90186-0 (glb)
[1. Bullies—Fiction. 2. Cousins—Fiction. 3. Grandmothers—Fiction. 4. Jealousy—Fiction. 5. Family problems—Fiction. 6. Moving, Household—Fiction. 7. Schools—Fiction. 8. Texas—Fiction.] I. Title: Laugh until you cry. II. Title.
PZ7.N65Lau 2004
[Fic]—dc22

2004009557

The text of this book is set in 11-point Trump Mediaeval.

Printed in the United States of America

November 2004

10 9 8 7 6 5 4 3 2

BVG

My gratitude to my teenage grandson, Matt Nixon, who served as my advisor and creator of the best of the humor in this book. Matt, who plans a career in cinema, made his debut as a stand-up comic at the age of twelve in West University police officer Mike Peterson's class. Next stop? Hollywood!

INTRODUCTION

Joan Lowery Nixon was a marvelous lady and a wonderful writer who well deserved her title: the grande dame of young adult mysteries.

I got to know Joan through the Mystery Writers of America at various seminars over the years, and of course at the annual MWA Edgar dinner, where the coveted Edgar was awarded to the best of the best. Four times Joan went up to collect an Edgar in the young adult field. Joan once told the story of how she stumbled across a mystery novel written for children when she was a little girl. She was so taken with the book that she promised herself that someday she too would write mysteries. How glad we are that she kept her promise.

Joan's love of mystery writing has been an inspiration to many young readers and writers alike. Joan also used her treasured time and talent not only to write more than 130 novels for children and young adults but also to work with young people to create projects that filled a need.

Joan was warm and charming and funny and caring. We were all saddened by her death in June 2003 and will miss her very much. It is good to know that because of her books she will never really leave us.

Mary Higgins Clark
Author of *The Cradle Will Fall*

CHAPTER ONE

Dodging low tree branches, leaping over dips and cracks in the sidewalk, Cody Carter ran harder and faster down Chimney Rock than he had ever run in his entire life. Someone was chasing him and quickly closing the short gap that lay between them.

The person yelled something, but fear and his own loud gasping for breath blocked Cody's ears, and he couldn't make out what was said. The only words that bounced through his brain were his: *I'm only thirteen years old. I'm too young to die.*

Ahead of him lay San Felipe, with cars backed up, waiting for the stoplight to change. In the nearest lane was a blue and white cop car, and Cody aimed for it, knocking on the passenger-side window. As he stared into the wide, surprised eyes of the uniformed policeman behind the wheel, Cody managed to croak, "Help!"

The officer flipped on his hazard lights and jumped from the car. Cody was bent over the fender, wiping rivulets of sweat from his eyes and gulping air.

"What's the matter, kid?" the officer called as he

walked around the front of his sedan. He placed a firm hand on Cody's arm. "Are you okay?"

Cody twisted to look over his shoulder. His cousin Hayden Norton had drifted back and was standing behind some of the solid, broad-limbed oak trees that lined the street. Hayden's buddy Bradley Lee was with him. They were both at least five inches taller than Cody, even though they were all the same age and in the same grade at school.

Hayden and Brad watched Cody warily, practically sniffing the air like a couple of dogs as they waited to see what would happen next. But Hayden's other sidekick, Eddie Todd, shorter and even sneakier, was quietly edging his way back along the street. It was just like Eddie to leave the others, Cody thought. If there was going to be trouble, Eddie wouldn't be in it, even though he probably started it.

"Those guys want to kill me," Cody told the officer. He straightened, able now to breathe more easily.

The officer smiled. "Take a poke at you, maybe, but are you really sure they want to kill you?"

The humor in his voice made Cody flinch. "They do," he insisted. "They said they were going to drag me back to school and stick my head in a toilet. Drowning somebody is killing them, isn't it?"

For the first time Cody craned his neck upward to take a good look at the policeman beside him. The man had to be at least six feet three, with broad shoulders. His dark eyes were crinkled at the outer corners, as if he were trying hard not to smile.

"What did you do to make them so mad at you?" The officer turned briefly, and Cody could see him sizing up Hayden and Brad. Eddie was long gone.

"I moved here," Cody answered. He pointed at Hayden, who was still peeking out from behind the trees. "That tall kid with the yellow hair and the big gut is my cousin Hayden. He just plain doesn't want me to be here."

"Where's here, besides Houston?"

"My grandmother's house. Hayden lives right next door. Mom and I came here to live with my grandmother because she's really sick."

"What's your grandmother's name?"

"Dorothy Norton."

"And where does she live?"

"On Longmont. I don't think it's too far from here."

The officer glanced back at Hayden and Brad. Then he opened the passenger-side door of his sedan. "Hop in," he said. "I'll give you a lift home."

Gratefully, Cody picked up his backpack and scrambled into the car, closing the door tightly behind him. He sneaked a quick look at Hayden, but the two boys had turned around and were strolling in the opposite direction.

As the officer started his patrol car, he said, "My name's Jake Ramsey. What's yours?"

"Cody Carter." Quickly he added, "Thanks for helping me out, Officer Ramsey."

"No problem. And call me Jake. It's easier to remember. Where are you from, Cody?"

"California. Santa Olivia." Cody heard the glumness in his voice and realized he was frowning.

Jake threw him a quick look. "I take it you'd rather be there right now than in Houston."

"Right," Cody answered. "My grandma's got something wrong with her heart. It beats out of rhythm, so my mom took a leave of absence from teaching kindergarten and came here to take care of her for a while. I had to come, too." Cody wiped sweat from his forehead and leaned back, thankful for the blast of cold from the air conditioner. "Texas is a lot different from California."

Jake nodded. "Sure, it's different, which is probably a good plan."

Cody shrugged. "If there was a plan, then Texas must have been Plan B."

Jake laughed. "You don't like Texas? I'm surprised. Most people like it. We get a lot of visitors. I read the other day that if you laid all the people who came to visit the Alamo end to end, the line would stretch around the world."

"And if you laid all the people who brag too much about Texas end to end . . ." Cody paused. "They'd deserve it."

Jake laughed again as he turned onto Longmont. "That's a good joke. Where'd you get it?"

Cody turned to him, surprised. "I didn't get it anywhere. I made it up." He pointed to an older, cream-trimmed one-story brick house, sandwiched between two large, more recently built two-story homes. "That's my grandmother's house."

Jake parked in front of the house and pulled out his wallet. "I'd like to buy your joke," he said.

"What do you mean, buy my joke?"

"I play sax and sit in with a combo most weekend nights at a club over on Richmond," Jake told Cody. "They usually have a stand-up comic for entertainment, and once a month they hold open-mike night, when anyone can try out a routine. I love my police work and I love playing music, but I've always wanted to be a comedian. The thing is, comedians need material. Good material. Jay Leno and David Letterman don't come up with their opening monologues on their own. They pay a whole bunch of writers to make up those jokes."

Cody was interested. He wasn't allowed to stay up late on school nights, but on Friday he stayed up long enough to hear the Top Ten List on *Letterman,* and on Saturdays his mom let him watch *Saturday Night Live.* "How come you want to be a stand-up comic?" he asked. It was hard enough for him to think of a cop as a musician. It was really stretching it to imagine a cop making people laugh! And Jake didn't look like a comic. He looked like what he was—a big, tough police officer.

"It's just something I'd like to try. I've always been a comedy fan. But I didn't realize how hard it would be to find good material. And even when you think you have good material, you might get a dead audience. I've seen it happen with some of the people who've taken a turn at open-mike night. I tried out a routine for some of the other officers, and I bombed. They told me I needed some new jokes."

He pulled a five-dollar bill out of his wallet. "I can't pay as much as the pros, but will this do?"

Cody smiled. "Sure. Thanks!" he said. It was five dollars more than he'd had five minutes ago. He put a hand on the door handle, but before he opened it he said, "I'm going to be a lawyer when I grow up, but I guess you could say I'm kind of a stand-up comic, too. At least, I was back home."

Jake's eyebrows rose, and Cody quickly said, "Not at a club or anything—just in school. Sometimes I'd get into trouble when I started joking in class, but I always made my friends laugh. Being funny was the only way to get through some of those classes."

Jake still looked skeptical. "But sometimes you got into trouble?"

Cody shrugged. "Sometimes the teachers laughed, too. But there were a few who never did."

"There's a time and a place for humor," Jake began. "When your teachers—"

Cody didn't let him finish. "I know that now. I haven't told any jokes here," he said.

"Not even to your friends?"

Cody slumped against the seat. "I don't have any friends in Houston."

"You do now," he said as they shook. "Here's my card. Call me if you want to talk." He picked up a notepad and pen. "And give me your grandmother's phone number so I can get in touch with you if I need more material. It's tough to put a good act together."

Cody left the patrol car feeling the best he'd felt since arriving in Texas. He'd not only found a new friend in Texas who laughed at his jokes, he'd even sold one of them! He liked making up jokes, and he'd never imagined he could make money selling them. Maybe he'd start typing his jokes on the computer and then printing—

His good feeling quickly left as he saw Hayden rounding the corner. Cody dashed the rest of the way into the house, slammed the door behind him, and dropped his backpack on the floor.

His mother appeared. "Cody! Please don't be so noisy. Your grandmother is sleeping! How many times do I have to remind you to come in quietly?"

"Sorry, Mom," Cody said sheepishly. He took a step toward her, expecting the hug with which she usually greeted him.

But she was frowning. "Why did you come home in a police car?" she asked.

It took Cody a moment to realize what his mother must have been thinking. He laughed. "Don't worry—I'm not in any trouble!" he tried to explain. "Jake—that's the officer's name—gave me a ride home. He's a musician and a cop, but what he really wants to be is a stand-up comic, and I told him a joke, and he liked it, and—"

"Cody," Mrs. Carter interrupted. "You're not answering the question I asked you. Why did you come home in a police car?"

Cody took a deep breath. "Hayden and his friends were chasing me," he said. "They were going to put my head in the toilet at school and drown me."

Mrs. Carter sighed. "Cody, I don't understand why you and your cousin can't get along and be friends. If you have any disagreements, surely you're old enough to talk things over with Hayden and work out the problem."

"While he's stuffing my head in a toilet?"

"He wouldn't do anything like that. You're letting your imagination get out of hand."

"My imagination? Mom, don't make me laugh."

Mrs. Carter walked over to a sofa and dropped onto it. She rested her head against the high back and for a moment closed her eyes. "I know it's difficult for you to be away from your friends and have to go to a new school. But, Cody, dear, your grandmother is ill, and I need your help and cooperation."

Cody sat next to his mother. "I'm sorry, Mom. I don't mean to get you mad."

"I'm not mad, and I'm not the one to worry about," Mrs. Carter told him. "It's your grandmother, Cody. Please get along with Hayden. It's important to Grandma. Do you understand?"

"Sure, Mom," Cody said. He tried to smile at her, but all he could think about was his cousin and what he could do to protect himself the next time he had to face Hayden. He was pretty sure Hayden didn't care about what was important to their grandmother.

CHAPTER TWO

Cody heard the light ring of the little silver bell on the nightstand in his grandmother's room.

His mother pulled herself to her feet and held out a hand to him. "Grandma's awake," she said. "I know she'll want to see you. As soon as she's ready, would you like a short visit with her?"

"Sure, Mom," Cody said. Living so far away, he had only seen his grandmother at holidays until this visit, but she had always been fun, and he loved her.

Cody waited until his mother called to him, then walked quietly into his grandmother's dimly lit bedroom. The bright-eyed, slightly plump woman, who had taken him on roller coaster rides at Astroworld, taught him about penguins at Moody Gardens' aquarium, and helped him stand in the dinosaur footprints at the Museum of Natural Science, seemed to have shrunk into a smaller, paler copy of herself.

Cody gulped and tried not to show what he was thinking. Every time he saw his grandmother, he felt the same sick jolt. Grandma shouldn't look like this. Grandmothers were supposed to stay the same and not change.

Dorothy Norton smiled from her bed and held out a hand.

Cody tiptoed to her, carefully holding her paper-dry fingers as if they might break. "Hi, Grandma," he whispered.

"Hi, Cody," she said, her eyes twinkling. "Why are you whispering? Is someone asleep?"

Cody laughed. "I thought I had to be quiet," he said.

"That's a change." She giggled. "When you were little, you liked to jump up and down on my bed and yell."

"I remember!"

She squeezed his fingers. "I'm sorry we've always lived so far apart. We didn't get to spend nearly enough time together. I'd like to have taught you to play chess and to Rollerblade, as I did with Hayden."

Cody felt a weird twist in his stomach and knew it must be jealousy. Of course his grandma had spent much more time with Hayden, who lived right next door. And because she knew Hayden a lot better than she did him, she probably loved Hayden more, too. Being Hayden's grandmother, she wouldn't think of him as the snot-nosed bully he really was.

"What happened today that was interesting?" Mrs. Norton asked.

Cody sat on the edge of the bed and smiled. His grandma never asked things like "How was school today?" or "Did you have a nice day?" She asked questions that people wanted to answer.

"I met this really neat police officer who's also a musician and who wants to be a stand-up comic," Cody said. Leaving out his reason for meeting Jake Ramsey, Cody found himself telling his grandma about the Texas joke and Jake's paying cash for it.

"You know what a stand-up comic is, don't you?" he asked.

Mrs. Norton laughed. "Of course! Jay Leno, Robin Williams, Chris Rock. Is this guy Jake Ramsey funny?"

"I don't know," Cody said.

"I've got some old *Reader's Digest* magazines in the garage," she said. "Maybe you can find some jokes he'd like in those."

"No, Grandma," Cody explained. "Comics have to use original stuff, not somebody else's material."

"Was that joke you told me about Texas original?"

"Yes," Cody said. "Sometimes I make up jokes."

"Wow!" Mrs. Norton said. "Not many people can do that. It's a special talent."

Cody smiled, feeling proud of himself. At least his grandma appreciated what he could do, even if Hayden and the other kids didn't. He would bet that Hayden couldn't make up jokes. Hayden probably had enough trouble just making up his mind to get up in the morning.

"How are you doing in English class?" Mrs. Norton asked.

Cody gave a start. "Fine," he said. "Well, not exactly fine. Maybe okay." He sighed. "Not exactly okay, either. Ms. Jackson's kind of hard."

"Ms. Jackson? I used to know all the English teachers when I taught English at Farnsworth. But I don't know a Ms. Jackson."

"She's new this year," Cody said. "She's a lot younger than most of those other teachers, Grandma. Some of them have probably been teaching there a hundred years, but Ms. Jackson told us she's only been a teacher for two."

He sighed. "She's making us read *Hamlet.* She said it was time we learned to appreciate William Shakespeare."

"That's not a bad idea," Mrs. Norton told him.

Cody shook his head. "People in Texas talk different than people in California, but at least I can understand what they're saying. Shakespeare wrote in English, so the words look right, but the way he put them together hardly makes any sense at all."

"Maybe I can help you," Mrs. Norton said. "I haven't been retired that long. Bring me your book and we can go over anything that's troubling you."

Cody hopped up from the bed just as his mother appeared in the doorway. "I think you've been visiting with Grandma long enough, Cody," she said. "We don't want to tire her."

"But Grandma is going to help me with my English homework," he complained.

"Not right now." Mrs. Carter's tone was firm. "Later."

"Later, Cody," Mrs. Norton echoed. For a moment she closed her eyes, and he could see the exhaustion on her face.

Dejected, he walked into the living room, picked up his backpack, and dumped the contents on the coffee table. For a moment he panicked. Where was his paperback copy of *Hamlet*?

With a sick feeling, he dropped into a nearby chair. He must have left the book in his locker at school. He had meant to put it in his backpack, but he'd seen Hayden heading his way, and he'd been in a hurry to escape. He had no choice about what to do next. He couldn't skip reading his homework or he'd be in big trouble. He'd have to race back to school and get the book.

Cody paused at the door to his grandmother's room

and whispered, "Mom? I'm going out. I'll be back in a few minutes."

As he stepped out the front door, he looked carefully in both directions, but there was no sign of Hayden, Brad, or Eddie. They were probably holed up in his aunt and uncle's backyard shed, which they'd turned into their secret clubhouse.

"You keep out," Hayden had said the first time his parents had invited Cody and Mrs. Carter over. "The clubhouse is our secret and none of your business."

Cody was only too glad to keep out. He wanted no part of anything his cousin was into—secret or not. It didn't make any difference to him what dumb stuff Hayden kept in that shed.

It was only six blocks to the Oliver J. Farnsworth Middle School, three blocks south of San Felipe. Cody set off at a jog, wishing he could have brought his bike with him from California. The hot late-September sun beat against his neck and shoulders, and he longed for the cool breezes that blew off the Pacific Ocean in Santa Olivia.

When Cody arrived at the massive redbrick building, the heavy front doors were locked. He peered inside through one of the big side windows and saw that the central hallway was empty.

The cleaning staff must be there, he thought. Maybe he could find one of them and they'd let him in. He walked around the building until he came to the west side. He saw some narrow steps, partly hidden on each side by large, spreading ligustrum bushes. They led down a half flight to a door. Hoping it was open, Cody tried the handle, but it was locked. *Shoot,* he thought. *How am I going to get in the building to get my book?* He cupped his hands against the glass panel in the door, trying to see inside.

The door opened so suddenly that Cody was thrown off balance. A hand gripped his shoulder, and an angry voice said, "Just what are you doing here?"

Cody looked up into the frowning face of a woman in dark slacks and blouse, with a lanyard and whistle draped around her neck. "I left one of my books in my locker," he said. "I came back to get it."

"You know the rules. No students allowed in the school past five p.m. unless they have legitimate business here."

"I have legitimate business," Cody said. "I need to get a book I accidentally left in my locker so I can do my homework."

The woman studied him. "You don't sound like you're from around here," she said. "Are you a student at Farnsworth?"

"Yes," Cody said. "But I'm new this semester. I'm from California. I came here with my mom, to live with and take care of my grandmother."

"What's your name?"

"Cody Carter. My grandmother Dorothy Norton used to teach here."

The tightness in the teacher's face softened. "I'm Coach Anderson," she said, "and I know your grandmother well. Where is this book you need, Cody?"

"In my locker."

She nodded. "I'll go with you to get your book. But after this, remember the rules. We can't continue to make exceptions."

"Thanks," Cody mumbled, not sure what else he should say. He stepped inside the building, which reeked of pine-scented cleanser. He followed the coach past the open door of a janitor's closet and up six steps to the silent hallway. From there it was a short distance to his locker. He couldn't help feeling like a prisoner marching with a warden. His fingers fumbled with the dial on his combination lock, and twice he went past the right numbers.

Finally, he managed to open his locker. He took out his copy of *Hamlet* and turned the dial, locking it again.

Once again they made their silent march down the hallway, and he stepped outside with a sigh of relief.

"Thanks," he called, but the door had shut and the coach had disappeared. He stood for a moment in the small, shaded space, enjoying the sense of being hidden from the rest of the world by the overgrown bushes, but he realized it was getting late and he had a lot of homework to do. He went down the few steps and started for home at a trot.

Cody was too hot and tired to jog very far, but he walked briskly, book in hand, his mind returning to Officer Jake Ramsey and his need for jokes. He liked the idea of earning money for making up jokes.

How about food? Everybody thinks about food. Fast food. Hamburgers. What would a stand-up comic say? Maybe . . . The government says we're all getting too fat. We have to give up hamburgers and start eating broccoli and spinach and string beans instead. Try telling that to my cousin Hayden. He thinks the four food groups are Hamburger, Cheeseburger, Chiliburger, and Coke.

And speaking of broccoli . . . modern science has discovered that you can count on broccoli doing three important things for you. It strengthens your muscles, brightens your vision, and leaves green stuff between your front teeth.

Suddenly, as Cody turned onto the block where his

grandmother lived, someone leaped out at him from a bush, and an arm was thrown around his neck. He was jerked backward, and his book was snatched from his hand.

"Hamlet," Hayden said with a sneer as he examined it. "Don't tell me you're going to study it tonight? I didn't think you could read."

"Give it back," Cody demanded. He ducked and twisted and pulled away from Eddie's grip.

"What did you tell that cop?" Brad asked.

"Yeah," Eddie said. "How come he drove you home? What did you tell him about us?"

"None of your business," Cody answered.

Brad took a step forward, but Cody jumped sideways. "For your information, I told him a couple of jokes," Cody said. He tried to smirk the way Hayden did, but he wasn't sure he was doing it right. "He told me they were funny and he paid me five dollars for them."

"That's dumb," Hayden said, and the others laughed. "Do you actually think we'd believe that somebody would pay *you* for telling him a joke?"

"He would. He did. He wants to be a stand-up comic, and he said he needed some good material."

Hayden joined in the laughter. "Don't expect us to believe that. He's not a stand-up comic. He's a cop."

"He's a musician, too. On some weekends he plays sax with a band at a club on Richmond."

The boys stopped laughing and looked at each other.

"I didn't think police officers could do anything like . . . well, you know, anything except be police," Eddie said.

Cody heard someone call Hayden's name. He looked up with the others and saw Alma Gomez, the Nortons' full-time housekeeper, standing on their front porch, waving.

"Come home, Hayden," Alma shouted. "Your mama wants you. Now."

Hands on hips, she stood without moving, watching them, and Cody breathed a sigh of relief. Hayden wouldn't try doing anything he shouldn't in front of Alma.

"Give me my book," Cody told Hayden, but Hayden tucked it inside his shirt and made a dash for home.

Brad and Eddie ran off in the opposite direction.

There was nothing for Cody to do but to follow Hayden to his house. The Nortons' front door was shut by the time Cody arrived, so he rang the bell.

Alma answered and smiled at him. "Hi, Cody. Can you come back later? Hayden's going out to dinner with his mama and dad, and he's supposed to get ready."

Desperate to get his book back, Cody said, "I'll just be a minute. I need to get my book for English class from Hayden."

Alma stepped aside, allowing Cody to walk into the beautiful entry hall, with its highly polished wood and curved staircase to the second floor.

Hayden appeared at the top of the stairs. He leaned on the banister and grinned down at Cody. "I don't have your book, dork," he said. "You must have left it at school."

Cody gulped. He had to get his book back. But how? He couldn't fight Hayden for it. Hayden would have him down flat and would be sitting on him within two minutes. He'd already done it more than once.

Cody took a deep breath and smiled at Alma. "I know where I left my book," he said. "In the clubhouse in the backyard. I'll just run out and get it."

"Okay," Alma said.

"No! It's not okay! Nobody goes in that clubhouse!"

Hayden ran down a dozen steps, but Alma held up a hand.

"Cody needs his book. He knows where it is. There's no reason why he can't go there and get it."

For just an instant Cody caught a flash of what seemed to be alarm in Hayden's eyes. Then Hayden slipped the book out from under his shirt. "Hey, Cody, you know I was kidding about your book being at school. Here it is. I found it where you dropped it and was just about to take it over to Grandma's to give it to you."

He tossed the book high in the air, and Cody scrambled to catch it. "Thanks," he said, aware that Alma was paying attention.

"Anytime," Hayden answered.

Alma looked at her watch. "Hayden, you better hurry. Your mama isn't going to like your being late."

"Thank you," Cody said, smiling at Alma. Clutching his book tightly, he hurried out the door and across the lawn to his grandmother's house.

He puzzled over the look on Hayden's face when the clubhouse had come up. There was obviously something inside the shed that Hayden didn't want anyone to see. Cody couldn't help wondering—what could it be?

CHAPTER THREE

Cody was sitting at the kitchen table, bent over the page in front of him, scowling, when his mother came into the room. As she opened the refrigerator and took out a package of lamb chops, she stopped to study him. "Why the unhappy face?"

"It's not just my face that's unhappy. It's all of me," Cody said. "Why did Shakespeare make everything he wrote so confusing? Why didn't he just write in plain English?"

"He did. It's the way the English language was spoken at that time."

"Too bad for me," Cody said.

"You're getting into Shakespeare a little early," Mrs. Carter said. "I think I was in tenth grade when our class read *Hamlet.*"

"Ms. Jackson loves Shakespeare. She said the sooner we learned to enjoy the poetry in his writing, the better." Cody made a face.

"Everybody reads Shakespeare sooner or later."

"Later sounds a lot better than sooner."

Mrs. Carter put the chops on the broiler tray and sprinkled them with garlic salt. "Do you remember when I rented the movie version of *Hamlet*? Maybe you'd like to see it again."

"No thanks. It was bad enough the first time. I knew it wasn't going to be a success or make any money."

"How could you know that?"

"There couldn't be a sequel. Everybody died in the end."

Mrs. Carter smiled and shook her head. "Exactly what bothers you about the play?" she asked.

"For one thing," Cody answered, "Hamlet goes around talking to himself all the time."

"When he talks to himself, it's called a soliloquy."

"Whatever it's called, it doesn't make a whole lot of sense to me. When Ms. Jackson reads what he says and asks what it means, I'm completely lost."

Mrs. Carter set the broiler timer, pulled out a chair facing Cody, and sat, propping her elbows on the table. "Maybe you should approach this in a different way. Instead of translating each word, try to understand the character of Hamlet."

"What's there to understand? I think he's a nutcase."

"He has been called 'the melancholy Dane.' "

"How come people from Denmark are called Danes? Shouldn't they be called Dens? Or Marks? I mean, I've heard of Great Danes, but they're dogs, and—"

"Stop trying to make a joke, Cody," his mother said. "Now think about why Hamlet is melancholy. He's lost his father."

"I lost mine, too," Cody said quietly. It had been four years since his father got sick and died.

"I know," Mrs. Carter said, "I miss your dad, too. It's been hard lately, especially now with Grandma . . ." Mrs.

Carter reached across the table and patted Cody's arm. "But that's why you might really find Hamlet's problems interesting."

She straightened and took a long, deep breath. "Now, let's get back to your homework. Remember, Hamlet knows he's the rightful heir and should rule Denmark, but his uncle Claudius has stolen control of both the kingdom and Hamlet's mother, the queen. Claudius wasted no time marrying Gertrude after the king's death. On top of all that, the ghost of Hamlet's father has appeared and told Hamlet that Claudius was the one who murdered him. The ghost wants Hamlet to avenge his death. It's a lot for Hamlet to handle. Not just the loss of his father—his life as he knew it. Everything is changed violently. Can you understand why Hamlet is sad and confused?"

"Do you think being sad is a good enough reason to go around whacking people and talking to a weird old skull in the cemetery and himself?"

Cody's mother rested her chin on her hands and sighed. "I suppose. I think poor Hamlet's feelings must have been unbearable."

The bell in Mrs. Norton's room sounded, and Mrs. Carter began to rise wearily. But Cody jumped up, putting a hand on her shoulder. "Stay here, Mom," he said. "I'll go find out what Grandma needs."

As he hurried into his grandmother's bedroom, she looked up at him from her pillows and smiled. "Just the person I wanted to see," she said. "You were going to come and talk to me about *Hamlet.* I've been waiting for you."

Cody sat on the small chair next to the bed. "Mom and I were just talking about that. Mom said Hamlet was unbearably sad. Do you think that's why he acted the way he did?"

"Oh, he was sad, all right," Mrs. Norton said. "But I believe that most of his actions were a result of the terrible things that had happened to him. He wasn't thinking normally. In the language of our times, he was mentally disturbed."

"Does that mean you think he was crazy?"

"His actions certainly were not normal."

Cody sighed. He was getting nowhere. His mom and grandmother couldn't even agree on what *Hamlet* was all about. He remembered that Hamlet, in one of his soliloquies, wished that his "too too solid flesh would melt." Cody also wished it had—along with the whole darned play.

"Would you like to get your book and read some of it to me?" Mrs. Norton asked.

Cody sighed. "It's hard for me to understand the play in the first place. If it's such a great play, you'd think people would agree on why Hamlet did the things he did."

Mrs. Norton smiled eagerly. "That's why the play is so much fun to discuss. Is Hamlet hero or victim? We can't view Hamlet, or anyone else for that matter, as totally good or totally bad."

"My dad could have figured it out," Cody said. "When Dad went before the court, he had to prove that the defendant was wrong. That's what an attorney does all the time."

"Your dad was proving only that the defendant was wrong in one particular case. Now, if you'll get your book . . ."

That was the last thing Cody wanted to do. He changed the subject. "Grandma," he blurted, "tell me about Uncle Austin and Aunt Rosalie. Even though they live right next door to you, it seems like they're always either out or going out. I hardly ever see them. I know

Uncle Austin is Mom's older brother, but I don't know much else."

Mrs. Norton looked surprised. "I guess Austin and Rosalie do stay busy most of the time. Austin is a very successful attorney. His type of work is different from what your father did. He works long hours and travels all over the world. Rosalie's volunteer jobs at the hospital and the Museum of Fine Arts take up a great deal of her time. And, of course, together and separately they have important social engagements. I understand and don't expect them to change their lives for me. It's only recently that I've needed some help."

Cody remembered overhearing his mom say on the phone, "If Rosalie could stop going to so many luncheons and parties, she could help take care of my mother."

Cody had had dinner with the Nortons shortly after he and his mom had arrived in Houston. Aunt Rosalie had asked him a question right after he'd taken a bite of roast beef. Cody remembered chewing fast and gulping before he answered.

"Hayden, dear, I hope you're noticing what good table manners Cody has," Aunt Rosalie had said. "Unlike you and your friends, Cody does not talk with his mouth full."

She'd smiled approvingly at Cody and added, "I've pointed out to Hayden that he could use you as a good example, Cody. You always remember to say 'please' and 'thank you,' too."

Hayden glared at Cody, who wished he could slide under the table. Maybe he should tell them that his mom drilled him before every family visit about what to say and do, under penalty of being grounded forever.

Aunt Rosalie began describing how they were going to decorate the luncheon tables at a fund-raising party she was in charge of. Cody was no longer of interest to her, but she'd only added to Hayden's bad attitude.

"Uncle Austin and Aunt Rosalie don't come over here very often, do they?" Cody asked his grandmother. He pressed his lips together tightly, wishing he hadn't been so blunt.

"No, but since I retired from teaching, I've spent a great deal of time with their sons, your cousins." Mrs. Norton smiled. "I miss Bennett, although I'm sure he's enjoying his first year at Harvard. I miss Hayden, too. I don't see him nearly as often as I used to. He's busy with school and sports. I can understand that."

He's busy with his thug buddies, Cody thought. "Have you ever been in Hayden's clubhouse?"

"Not since he turned it into a clubhouse," Mrs. Norton answered. "It began life as a potting shed and a place to protect plants that couldn't take the winter freezes. I think Austin still uses it for gardening and keeps some tools and fertilizer in it, but I suppose there's plenty of space to add a few chairs and whatever else a clubhouse needs." She studied Cody. "Hasn't Hayden invited you into the clubhouse yet?"

"Not exactly," Cody said.

"I'm sure he will. Give him a little time," Mrs. Norton said. "It makes me happy to realize that you and Hayden will finally get to know each other as friends, as well as cousins. You're in some of the same classes, and you can enjoy the school activities together. The football season should be starting soon, shouldn't it?"

"There's a game on Friday."

Mrs. Norton's smile was so bright that Cody gulped. His mother was right. There was no way he could let his grandmother know what a no-good bully Hayden was.

And he couldn't really complain to her about having to be in Texas. She was his grandmother.

Cody struggled to think of the right thing to say. He was saved by his mother's appearance in the doorway. Bustling past him to the bed, she said, "Mom, your dinner's almost ready. Let me prop you up against your pillows. Cody, wash up and head for the kitchen."

"Cody, after you've eaten, come back and bring your book. We'll go over your reading assignment," Mrs. Norton said.

"Thanks, Grandma. See you later," Cody answered, and left the room. But at the door to the kitchen, he paused.

Lamb chops and *Hamlet* lay ahead of him. He could handle the lamb chops, even though they were not his favorite things to eat. But *Hamlet*? How was he ever going to manage that?

CHAPTER FOUR

In the morning Cody's mother handed him her cell phone. "Grandma's doctor is going to call later today, after he's seen the results of her latest blood test," she said. "There's a good chance he might give her a prescription for a new medication he's thinking of trying. Call me right after school. You know where the drugstore is, right down on Westheimer. You can stop by and pick it up on your way home."

"Okay, Mom," Cody said. He slipped the phone into the pocket of his blue polo shirt. He hoped the new medicine would help his grandma.

English class came right before lunch. Cody slid into his assigned seat in the row near the window, his stomach rumbling. He pretended he didn't see Hayden stroll into the room with Eddie and Brad.

Hayden began to swagger toward Cody, but at that moment Ms. Jackson came into the room and Hayden headed to his seat. The bell rang, and Ms. Jackson shut the door. She wore a neat dark blue jacket and skirt, and round silver earrings dangled from her ears. She didn't look like a teacher, Cody thought. Instead, she looked like an anchorwoman on TV. He'd never seen her in jeans and wondered if she even owned a T-shirt. She had decorated her classroom more than most of the other teachers, and Cody realized that even though he wasn't enjoying *Hamlet,* he liked Ms. Jackson and the extra effort she made. He leaned back in his seat, gripping his copy of the play, and tried to prepare himself for class.

"Good morning, everyone," Ms. Jackson said. She silently checked the rows to make sure every seat was filled, then put down the clipboard she was holding. "Did everyone read Act Five, Scene Two, the last scene in the play?"

Without waiting for an answer, she said, "We'll talk about that scene in a few minutes. But first, I want to discuss projects with you."

Cody saw that he wasn't the only one who was instantly alert. "What projects?" someone asked.

"The projects you're going to do to complete our study of *Hamlet,*" she said. "Instead of a test. You'll enjoy this assignment," Ms. Jackson told the class, "because you'll have a chance to use your creativity."

Ignoring another groan and a couple of grumbles, she continued. "If you can't come up with an original idea, then you might like to write a two-page theme about one of the topics I've listed on the board. For example, you could discuss Polonius's advice to his son, Laertes, or you might write about the two appearances of the ghostly king.

"On the other hand, I'm hoping that some of you might like to construct a diorama of one of the major scenes in the play, or paint a picture, or think of something different and unusual to do. What you create will be up to you." Ms. Jackson picked up an old leather book wrapped in plastic. "I've brought in something special to inspire you. This is a very old, rare edition of *Hamlet.* It's quite different from the paperback edition we've been reading. On Friday I will give everyone a chance to look at it."

Hayden raised his hand. "Is it worth a lot of money?"

"Why, I suppose it is, Hayden. But it has more of a sentimental value for me. It's been in my family for generations. You may work on your projects on your own, or you can choose a partner and combine your talents." There was a buzz throughout the room as most of the kids immediately tried to connect with their friends.

Cody watched for a moment, then reached across the aisle and tapped a redheaded girl named Jennifer. He didn't like feeling left out, and Jennifer seemed to do well in class. He wouldn't mind doing a project with her.

She whirled toward him, waiting to see what he wanted.

"Do you want to work with me?" Cody asked.

"I'm sorry. I can't," Jennifer said, trying to look sorry but failing. "I already promised Emily."

Cody shrugged. "Okay," he said. As Jennifer turned her back on him again, Cody slumped in his seat. He wished the doctors would find the right medicine for Grandma so she'd get better soon. He missed his real school in Santa Olivia. He missed his friends. He wanted to go back home.

Ms. Jackson's voice broke into his thoughts. "This is Tuesday. Your project won't be due until Friday, so you'll have three evenings to work on it. Any questions?"

Emily Estrada waved her hand high in the air, and when Ms. Jackson looked in her direction, she said, "There's a football game on Friday after school, and the cheerleaders have to practice."

"You'll have time to do both. The project won't take that much time."

Jennifer raised her hand. "How much is the grade on the project going to count toward our final grade?" she asked.

Ms. Jackson's gaze took in the entire class. "It will be important for your final grade."

"Ten percent? Twenty?"

Ms. Jackson walked to her desk and picked up her copy of *Hamlet,* opening it to the last scene. "I have a creative idea," she said. "Why don't you work on the project as if it were going to be worth one hundred percent? Now, let's open our books to page 133, Act Five, Scene Two. Hamlet and Horatio are talking. Who'd like to read Hamlet's dialogue, beginning with 'Sir, in my heart'? Brad?"

Brad slid down in his seat, mumbling, "I didn't have time to do my homework."

"See me after class," Ms. Jackson said quietly. "Emily?"

Cody silently read along with Emily, glad that his grandmother had explained that "mutines in the bilboes" meant "mutineers in fetters in prison" and "plots do pall" meant "plans fail." Otherwise, he might as well have been reading in another language. Emily finished, giving a flip of her long, dark ponytail, and Ms. Jackson said, "Thank you. Now let's see who can tell us what Hamlet was saying."

Cody bent over, shrinking as small as he could.

He let out such a loud sigh of relief when Hayden was called on that Jennifer turned and stared at him, and Ms. Jackson looked at him with surprise.

"Hayden, can you tell us what Hamlet was describing when he said the following?

Methought I lay
Worse than the mutines in the bilboes."

For a moment Hayden was silent. Cody slid up straight and raised his head. He actually knew the answer! He and his grandma had discussed it.

But Hayden answered, "Bilboes were metal cuffs that were put around prisoners' wrists and ankles and fastened them to the chains in the wall in dungeons. And mutines were mutineers, so they were lying in prison wearing these bilboes. And Hamlet said he was even worse off than they were, which was really bad."

"Excellent answer, Hayden," Ms. Jackson said. "I can see you made good use of the footnotes in the last pages of the book."

Cody started. There were footnotes? If Ms. Jackson had told the class about them, then he must have been thinking about something else. He'd only read the pages that were assigned and had seen no reason to look in the back of the book.

As Hayden smirked at Cody, he got that weird feeling in the pit of his stomach again. He supposed he was jealous of Hayden, and he tried to push the feeling away.

But Ms. Jackson walked to the window side of the room and smiled at him. "All right, Cody. You're eager to answer. Suppose you take the next lines:

Rashly
(And praised be rashness for it) let us know,
Our indiscretion sometime serves us well
When our deep plots do pall."

Cody felt as though a giant eraser had swept through his mind. It was a total blank. What had his grandma told him?

"To begin with, what does 'rashness' mean?" Ms. Jackson prompted.

" 'Rashness' . . . uh . . . oh, doing something without, uh, thinking about it first, like whether or not it was a good idea," Cody stammered.

"That's right. So take it from there. Why did Hamlet say 'praised be rashness'?"

Cody stared at the page. "They . . . uh . . . did something without thinking about it, which was rash, but rashness works out okay when plots pall . . . uh, fail. If their plots fail."

He shifted in his seat, and his book fell to the floor with a crash.

Jennifer gave a loud sniff and rolled her eyes, and he heard Hayden snicker.

As Cody bent to pick up his book, his face flushed hot. He knew it was probably bright red and he'd made everything even worse. But he straightened up to see Ms. Jackson walking to the other side of the room.

She said, "Thank you, Cody. You're on the right track." Then she read:

"There's a divinity that shapes our ends,
Rough-hew them how we will."

She called on a kid named Paul, and he began to answer. Paul seemed nice enough. Cody had seen him drawing pictures—especially of horses—all over his notebook. Cody tried to listen, but all he could think about was how he had stumbled through a really dumb answer. Hayden would probably never let him forget it.

When the lunch bell rang, Cody headed to his locker. He pulled his lunch bag from the shelf, but he didn't hurry with the others toward the cafeteria. He saw Hayden's

Stupid Squad up ahead, waiting for him. Wanting only to be alone, Cody walked down the hall in the opposite direction and slipped out the side door he'd discovered the day before. He sat on the bottom step of the small alcove, resting his back against the cement wall. It was cool in the shade, in spite of the Texas heat.

He munched on the peanut butter and jelly sandwich his mother had made for him and thought about his home and school in Santa Olivia. Tears blurred his vision, and he rubbed angrily at his eyes with the back of one hand. He wasn't going to cry. Not here! Not now!

For what seemed like a long time, Cody leaned against the wall and thought about the good old days in Santa Olivia. Suddenly he jumped as the electronic bell over the door slammed against his ears in a rapid beat.

A fire drill? At lunchtime?

He was tempted to stay where he was, but he knew that would just mean trouble, so he got to his feet and began to jog around the corner of the building toward the quadrangle in back, where the classes were supposed to line up during emergency drills.

As he entered the gate, Cody ran straight into Coach Anderson, who grabbed his shoulders to steady him. She didn't let go, but stared down at him, checking him over, inch by inch. She frowned at the phone clip on his pocket. "What are you doing out here?" she demanded.

"I was eating lunch," Cody said. "I brought it today. My lunch sack—" He glanced down at his empty hands. "I guess I left it on the stairs."

"On the stairs is not in the cafeteria, where *all* students are supposed to eat lunch," she said. "Even though you're a new student, you should know that."

"I do know," Cody said. He tried to shrug but couldn't

since she still had a grip on his shoulders. "I—I just felt like being alone."

The bell kept up its insistent clamor, and Cody's head began to hurt.

Coach Anderson stepped back, dropping her arms. "Hurry. Get in line with your class. Every student has to be accounted for."

Cody took off at a run and skidded to a stop at the end of the lines in front of Ms. Jackson, who was also his homeroom teacher. "What's with the fire drill at lunchtime?" he asked Jennifer, who was standing next to him, but at that moment the bell went silent.

The principal of Farnsworth Middle School, Mr. Carmody, spoke to the students using a portable hand mike. "A few minutes ago," he announced, "through an anonymous telephone call to our main office, we received a bomb threat."

One of the girls gave a little shriek, and everyone started talking. Mr. Carmody had to shout twice for silence so he could continue.

"The police have arrived, and the school will have to be searched." He paused, then added, "I am counting on the likelihood that it was not one of our own students."

"We were all in the cafeteria," someone complained.

Cody saw Coach Anderson slowly turn and search the crowd until she spotted him. She approached Mr. Carmody, who held the microphone down as the coach leaned toward him and spoke quietly in his ear.

Then he turned and stared at Cody, too.

Cody gulped as he realized what they must be thinking. *It wasn't me!* He wanted to shout, but he couldn't. He hadn't been accused, so he couldn't say anything.

He saw Officer Jake Ramsey and another uniformed

officer step out of the building and walk to the principal's side. They spoke for a few minutes, and then Jake turned and looked at Cody, too.

Cody's legs felt so weak it was hard to keep standing. He tried taking a deep breath to steady himself, but it was difficult to breathe.

Mr. Carmody picked up the mike. "The police estimate that it will take at least three hours to thoroughly search the school building," he said. "So we will proceed with early dismissal. Please remain where you are while arrangements are made."

Then, once again, he looked directly at Cody. "At this time," he said, "I would like Cody Carter to report directly to me."

CHAPTER FIVE

"I didn't do it," Cody said.

"He wasn't in the cafeteria, where he was supposed to be," Coach Anderson stated.

"Young man—" Mr. Carmody began, but Jake stepped forward. He was big enough to take charge, and his voice was firm. Even Coach Anderson kept quiet and paid attention.

"Before we jump to any conclusions, let's get the answers to some questions," Jake said. He turned to Cody. "Where'd you eat lunch, Cody?"

"On the steps outside the side door," Cody said.

"All students are supposed to eat in the cafeteria," the coach interrupted, but Jake gave her a hard look, and she stepped back.

Cody decided he'd better explain himself. "I—I didn't feel well. I wanted to be by myself, so I picked a quiet place where nobody would be."

"Nobody saw you there?" Jake asked.

Cody gulped. From what he had learned about law, he realized that Jake was asking whether there were any witnesses, anyone who could prove that Cody was there. Suddenly he remembered. "No, but I left my lunch bag on the steps. I meant to throw it away, but the bell rang and—"

"I'll go check," the other policeman said. He strode toward the corner of the building in the direction Cody pointed out.

Cody was aware that a lot of the kids were watching him. He heard Brad say loudly, "Nobody saw Cody after we got out of English class."

Eddie piped up, "That's 'cause he was—"

Hayden gave him a punch on his arm. "Don't interrupt," he muttered.

"Nobody saw you, either," Jennifer snapped, glaring at Brad.

"Yeah? Well, I had to see Ms. Jackson after class."

"Does your mom know you've got a phone with you?" Jake asked Cody.

"She gave it to me," Cody said. "The doctor is supposed to call her about a new medicine he might give my grandmother, and if he does, then she wants me to go to the drugstore and pick it up on my way home. I have to call Mom right after school and find out."

Jake nodded, as if he had accepted Cody's answer.

Jake's partner came back holding a lunch sack. "You left an apple in your lunch bag," he said to Cody. As he handed it to him, he reported to Jake, "It was right where he said it was."

"That doesn't mean anything. He could have made the call," Coach Anderson insisted.

"But I didn't," Cody said, close to panic. "I didn't call the school."

"We can check your school's incoming calls with the

phone company and find out within a few minutes if a call was made from Cody's phone," Jake said.

With trembling fingers, Cody took the phone from his pocket and handed it to Jake, but Jake gave it back to him. "We don't need your phone to do the checking. Before you go home, just call your mom as you were asked to do."

The coach looked from Mr. Carmody to Jake. "Aren't you going to do something?" she asked.

"Yes, ma'am. We're going to check your school's incoming phone calls, like I told you."

She looked at Cody. "I mean about Cody Carter."

"There's nothing to do right now. Prank phone threats to a school are nothing new. In an area as large as Houston, we usually get some every year."

"But what if this call wasn't a prank?"

"That's always a possibility. And that's why the bomb squad is here, and why we'll keep a close eye on your school for the next couple of weeks."

Mr. Carmody took a step forward. "It appears that all we can do at the moment is what the officer suggested, Ms. Anderson." He turned on his microphone again. "All students immediately get back in line so your homeroom teachers can take roll call."

While everyone began hurrying to get in place, Cody looked up at Jake. His stomach hurt, and he felt sick and scared. "I didn't have anything to do with a bomb threat," he insisted. "I wouldn't do a thing like that."

"I believe you," Jake said.

"But they think . . ." Cody couldn't finish.

"They won't if we prove them wrong."

"How are we going to do that?"

"By finding out who made the call," Jake told him.

"But how?"

"Just leave that up to us," Jake said.

Cody took a long breath, already feeling better. He turned, ready to join his class and get in line.

At that moment Ms. Jackson glanced at Cody and beckoned to him.

"What's your teacher's name?" Jake asked.

"Ms. Jackson. She's my English teacher and homeroom teacher, too," Cody said, and smiled weakly at Jake.

He walked quickly toward the others in his homeroom, surprised when he realized that Jake was not only walking with him but had a hand clamped on his shoulder, steering him toward Ms. Jackson.

As they stopped in front of her, Cody knew he couldn't just stand there looking stupid. He had to say something, so he introduced Jake.

Jake gave Ms. Jackson a broad smile. "There has been some confusion about who was where and when," he said. "I just want you to know that there is absolutely no evidence that Cody was involved in that phone call."

Ms. Jackson smiled back. "I'm glad to hear that," she said.

Jake's grip loosened, so Cody quickly slipped to one side and hurried to the end of the line.

He expected Hayden to get on his case, but to his relief, Hayden and the other two kids were intent on trying to hear what Jake was saying to Ms. Jackson.

"We can trace the call," Cody heard, and he saw Eddie throw Hayden a quick look.

Hayden ignored him and just kept staring at Jake.

Ha! Cody thought. *I know you guys would like the caller to be me, but tracing the call will prove that it wasn't.*

Jennifer was talking with Emily, so Cody could only pick up a word or two. He heard Jake say, "Prank calls have been going on for years. Nothing to worry about nine times out of ten." And he heard Ms. Jackson saying, "While we were in the teachers' lounge having lunch . . ."

Thankful that Hayden hadn't immediately begun to give him a bad time, Cody kept his eyes on Jake, too, and watched him stride back into the building.

Whatever Jake had said must have reassured Ms. Jackson, because for a while after he left, she kept on smiling.

An hour later Cody left the drugstore with the package for his grandmother. Warily, he glanced to each side as he walked toward Longmont, expecting to be jumped by Hayden and his buddies at any moment.

To his surprise, there was no sign of them, but as he turned onto Longmont, he saw a bright blue cop car parked in front of his house. Not knowing what to expect, Cody ran up the front steps and through the front door, coming to an abrupt stop just inside the living room as he faced Jake Ramsey.

Jake seemed to overflow one of the wingback chairs by the fireplace. He didn't get up, but he smiled at Cody, as did Mrs. Carter, who sat opposite him in the matching chair.

"Come in, honey. Sit down with us," she said. As Cody shoved his books onto the coffee table and handed the small bag from the drugstore to his mother, she added, "Officer Ramsey was kind enough to explain all about the prank call to your school today and what happened."

Cody turned to Jake. "It was just a prank? They didn't find a bomb?"

Jake shook his head. "No bomb. It was probably some kid with no brains or sense trying to scare everyone."

"It wasn't me, Mom," Cody said.

"Of course it wasn't," she answered.

Cody squirmed. "Coach Anderson thought that just because I wasn't in the cafeteria and because I had your phone with me, I had to be the one who made the call. But Officer Ramsey said they could trace the call to the school. He said they could prove I hadn't made it." He looked hopefully at Jake. "Did you trace it? Did you find out who made the call?"

Jake nodded. "We've learned it came from a pay phone outside a convenience store a block away from the school." Jake unfolded his long legs and stood. "Cody, I got your mom's permission for you to come with me tonight to a ball game. I'm pitching for one of the Houston police department's softball teams. We're playing a team from West University over in Memorial Park. I need someone to cheer for me, and maybe do a little work as batboy, too."

"Me? Sure, I'd like to go." Cody scrambled to his feet.

"Then get your homework done. I'll pick you up around five."

Excited about the evening to come, Cody said goodbye to Jake, paid a quick visit to his grandmother, and spread out his books on the kitchen table. He'd have time to finish his homework for every class except English, and he wasn't worried about that. He had only his project about *Hamlet,* which wasn't due until Friday.

For about an hour he worked steadily. When he stopped for a breather, a thought popped into his brain.

His mother had said it was a prank call. What did she think, really? Was the caller just some nut making a crank call or someone who intended to bomb the school?

Cody shuddered. His worst fear, however, was that everyone would keep thinking the caller was him.

CHAPTER SIX

Jake's own car was a ten-year-old Mercury Marquis, one of the long, stretched-out models that had gone out of style when most cars went either compact or SUV. Jake didn't seem to mind the age of his car, and Cody noticed that it fit him perfectly, with plenty of headroom and space for his long legs. He imagined Jake trying to squeeze himself into a Volkswagen bug or a little Beemer and couldn't help grinning.

"What's so funny?" Jake asked.

Cody was afraid that whatever he said would sound insulting to Jake and his car, so he answered, "I'm just feeling good, I guess."

Jake smiled back, then turned onto Shepherd, heading north. "Did you get your homework done?" he asked.

"Sure," Cody said. "Except for English. We don't have anything due tomorrow. We're just supposed to be working on a project about *Hamlet* that's due on Friday."

"Hamlet," Jake said. "I remember having to study *Hamlet*. He was one complicated guy."

"Mom said he was melancholy, but Grandma said he was crazy. I don't know which one is right."

"Want another opinion?"

"I guess," Cody said, although he really wished they could forget Hamlet and talk about something else.

"I think he pretended to be way off his rocker so that he could claim temporary insanity and not be blamed for what he'd done," Jake said. "I've seen plenty of perps pull that, and their defense attorneys go right along with it."

"What's a perp?"

"It's short for *perpetrator.* A perpetrator's the guy who commits the crime."

"Oh, I know—a defendant. My dad was a prosecutor—a district attorney." Cody smiled. "I bet anybody prosecuting Hamlet would get a sure conviction."

"Unless the jury believed the temporary insanity defense."

Cody thought about Hamlet. Had he been pretending to be crazy? Or was he really crazy? Or just sad? How was anybody supposed to figure this guy out? He gave a long sigh.

Jake threw him a quick glance. "Why don't we ask Ms. Jackson what she thinks?"

"She wants us to make up our own minds," Cody said. "She listed Hamlet's state of mind as one of the topics we could work on for our project." He suddenly realized what he had just heard. "You said *we.* What do you mean, *we* could ask her?"

"I mean *you* could ask her," Jake said. He turned onto the drive that led through Memorial Park. The path that paralleled the drive was crowded with walkers and joggers, keeping up a steady pace. "I'll be dropping by your school a couple of times a day for the next week, just to make sure everything's under control, and I was thinking it's likely I'll see her while I'm there."

Cody leaned back against the seat. For just an instant he closed his eyes. "It's because of the bomb threat," he said. "That's why you'll come by the school. You think the guy who telephoned will call again, don't you?"

"Nobody knows what the person will do," Jake said. "People who make calls like that are usually bored or carrying a grudge, or don't bother to think about what's right and what's wrong. Chances are he got his kicks from scaring everyone and that's the last we'll hear from him."

"What if it isn't?"

Jake pulled onto a side road and into a parking lot. Between the lot and the thick forest that lay beyond, Cody could see a baseball diamond, with four rows of bleachers at each side of home base. Grown-ups and kids, carrying coolers and soft drinks, were already beginning to fill the seats.

As Jake turned off the engine, he said, "Cody, we take precautions even when we think there's nothing to worry about. Stop worrying. You can take precautions, too."

Cody looked up, startled. "Like what?"

"Like making sure you're with the other kids all the time. Don't go off alone. Don't give anyone a chance to make a threatening call while you're not around and then point a finger at you. Got it?"

"Okay," Cody said.

"Then stop looking so unhappy." Jake swung open his car door. "Come on, we've got a ball game to win."

Cody followed Jake to the diamond, where he was introduced to a lot of friendly people whose names he'd never be able to remember.

"Cody's our batboy tonight," Jake announced, and he led Cody over to a spot near home base. "Be sure you stand far enough back so you won't get hit by a flying bat. Ever been batboy before?"

"No, but my dad used to take me to games, so I know what I'm supposed to do," Cody said. "Mostly, it's pick up the bat after the batter starts running, and put it on the rack with the others."

"Right. You'll do a good job."

Cody took a quick look around. "All these people are police officers?"

"Yes. And their families."

"Don't they have to be on duty in case somebody robs a bank, or runs his car through a red light, or whatever else perps do?"

Jake grinned. "The cops you see here have already put in a day's work. We're off duty. There are plenty of other officers out there, ready to go into action if they're needed."

Someone yelled, "Come on, y'all! Play ball!" and Jake gave Cody a pat on the shoulder and took off at a trot to join his team.

As Cody waited at one side, he thought about how the day had turned so completely upside down. The huge redbrick Oliver J. Farnsworth Middle School had been full of activity. Now it was empty and silent. The early-evening sun would be splashing the rows of reflecting windows with deep gold. Even Coach Anderson would have gone home by this time. If whoever had called earlier about a bomb wanted to do more than just make a threat, he could go to the school and sneak around to the back and . . .

The loud crack of a bat startled Cody. All thoughts of school problems disappeared as he joined in cheering for a tall, thin woman on Jake's team who had rounded first base and was heading for second.

The game was close, and it was fun. At one point Cody was sent in as pinch hitter when someone on the team turned his ankle. Cody swung wild on the first pitch. But on his second attempt to hit the ball out of the park, he barely tipped it, and it rolled into the field.

The catcher and third baseman both dove for the ball, colliding with each other, and Cody made it safely to first base.

Then Jake hit a homer, his team won, and the game was over. With a lot of laughter and good-natured teasing, everyone left the field, and another group arrived to start their game.

As the banks of bright lights on the field switched on, breaking the dusk that was settling around them, Jake held the car door open for Cody. "Time for food," he said. "Let's celebrate our win."

Cody peeled his sweaty T-shirt away from his chest, aware that Jake looked every bit as grungy. "We're kind of a mess," he said.

"Right. So we'll hit a Sonic Drive-In. They've got great burgers, huge onion rings, and chocolate shakes so thick you have to eat them with a spoon. It's the kind of food made to fill up hungry ballplayers like us."

Cody felt good about hanging out with Jake. "You could have been in pro ball if you'd wanted to be," he said.

"Maybe." Jake got into the car and turned the ignition key. "But I'm doing what I really want to do. From the time I wasn't much bigger than you, I planned to be in law enforcement." As he backed the car out of the parking lot and pulled onto Memorial Drive, he said, "Next month I'm going to take the exam for detective."

"What's the difference between being a policeman and being a detective?" Cody asked.

"There's a lot more to learn if you want to be a detective," Jake answered. "Detectives specialize in different types of crime, and they not only study how crimes are committed and solved, they also have to know as much as possible about the people who commit crimes—their motives and actions and even body language that might be clues to what they've been up to."

"What kinds of clues?"

"A guilty suspect could keep from looking you in the eye or not be able to stop twiddling his fingers or rubbing his nose."

"You mean looking nervous?"

"Right. But not all perps look or feel nervous. Some of them stay cool. So then you smoke 'em out. You ask a question repeatedly and try to trip them up and see if they give different answers, which could prove that they're lying. And, most important of all, you find the motive."

"You mean their reason for committing the crime?"

"That's it. There always has to be a motive."

They had gone under Loop 610 and were headed down Westheimer.

"The drive-in's not far from here," Jake said. "How about what I suggested? Burgers and all that good stuff okay with you?"

"It all sounds great," Cody said. He added, grinning, "Speaking of burgers, you ought to meet my cousin Hayden. He thinks the four food groups are Hamburger, Cheeseburger, Chiliburger, and Coke."

Jake laughed. "That's a good one. Got any more?"

"Sure," Cody said, and he told Jake his broccoli joke.

"Maybe I can use those," Jake said. "Sometime, if

you've got the time, I'll have to try my routine out on you."

Cody suddenly realized how hungry he was. But it really didn't matter what or where he ate. He was having a great time just being with Jake.

As Jake drove back to Cody's grandmother's house after dinner, he asked Cody, "So what's going on with this cousin of yours?"

"Let's not talk about Hayden. Let's talk about somebody who doesn't make me turn green and get sick to my stomach," Cody answered.

"I know you don't want to talk about it, but Hayden has been bullying you and I'd like to help. Nearly everyone has a bully in his life at some time or another. I wasn't always this big, you know. When I was a kid, I was the scrawniest one in the neighborhood. You better believe I got picked on. The trick is to be smarter than the bully."

Cody tried to imagine Jake as a scrawny kid. "It's just that Hayden is bigger than I am, and he has two mean, stupid friends who like to be bullies, too. Three against one."

"Right. But this isn't about being outnumbered. Using your fists is not going to solve this problem. You need to use your mind. Figure out why Hayden is giving you a bad time and then outsmart him."

"His motive?"

Jake smiled and said, "Yes! His motive. Then think of a way to solve the problem. I know things are tough for you right now, Cody, but hang in there." They pulled up to the house.

"Thanks, Jake! I had fun tonight." Cody shut the

door and sighed. He knew Jake was right, and he appreciated the advice, but he was still confused. How could he figure out what Hayden's motive was? Even if he knew, what good would it do?

He could really solve his problem with Hayden if a monster's slimy claw came out of the sky, grabbed Hayden by his fat head, and carried him off to another planet.

He let himself in, walked to the sofa, and flopped on it, facedown, quickly rubbing away a couple of tears that had escaped. He couldn't let go and cry.

He sat up, swung his feet to the floor, and took a deep breath to steady himself. "Hey, Mom," he said. "Wait till I tell you about the game. I got to pinch-hit and made it all the way to first base."

Mrs. Carter came out of the kitchen and joined Cody on the sofa. She put an arm around his shoulders and hugged him to her. "I'm glad you had a good time," she said. "I want to hear all about the game. But first, let me tell you before I forget: Grandma has a doctor's appointment and some tests late tomorrow afternoon, so when you get out of school, we won't be home. Instead of coming here, go over to Hayden's house. Aunt Rosalie said Alma would bake you something good for a snack so you and Hayden can do homework together."

Cody stiffened. "Mom, I don't have to go to Hayden's! I'm thirteen! I'm old enough to stay here by myself!"

"I know," she answered. "Rosalie is trying now to be helpful and Grandma was delighted with her offer. Go along with the plans, please, Cody. It will make things so much easier for all of us."

Cody nodded agreement, although it was the last thing in the world he wanted to do. "Okay," he said.

"Thanks, honey," Mrs. Carter said, and squeezed his shoulder. "Now, tell me about the ball game."

Cody described the park and the baseball diamond and the way Jake had slammed the ball out of the field, but he had a scared feeling in the pit of his stomach. If he wasn't careful, having a snack with a snake like Hayden could end up with Cody himself being the snack.

CHAPTER SEVEN

On Wednesday Cody did as Jake had cautioned. He made sure that while he was at school, he was never alone. Now and then he thought he saw some of the kids watching him with suspicion, but he pretended not to notice.

Lunchtime was the hardest. He bought the cafeteria lunch and balanced a tray containing dishes of something brown, something yellow, and something green, not paying much attention to what they were. Stopping by a table with two empty places, he began to put down his tray.

"Okay if I sit here?" he asked Emily, who sat across from Jennifer.

Emily looked up, flipping the end of her long ponytail back from her shoulder. "Those seats are saved," she said.

"No, they're . . . ," Jennifer began in surprise, but she stopped short as she glanced up, over her shoulder, at Cody. "Oh," she said. "Sorry. I forgot. They're saved."

Cody felt his face turn red with embarrassment. Without a word he walked to the far end of the cafeteria, away from Emily's loud whispers.

Plopping down his tray at the end of one of the tables, Cody kept his eyes on his food and began to eat.

A few minutes later Hayden slid onto the bench opposite him. Brad sat next to Cody, elbowing him to the end of their bench, and Eddie crowded in beside Brad.

"Made any more interesting phone calls lately?" Hayden asked Cody in a voice loud enough so that the kids around them could hear.

Cody put down his fork. With his tongue, he pried away the gluey macaroni and cheese that was stuck to the back of his front teeth, then said, "You know I didn't make that call."

Hayden leaned close, and Brad did, too. Eddie just grinned. "What call?" Hayden asked, his eyes wide with faked innocence.

"You're my cousin, you know. We have the same grandmother. Why don't you just leave me alone?" Cody asked.

"That's no fun," Hayden said, really annoyed.

Cody polished off the milk that was left in his carton. "Let's talk about something else," he said.

"Like what? Like your *Hamlet* project? You couldn't find anyone to work with, could you?"

"It doesn't make any difference."

"Sure it does." Hayden grinned and added, "It does make a difference. So we're cousins, and I have to look out for you. I even have to babysit you this afternoon while your mama's not home."

Cody heard a snicker behind him. He didn't know who was enjoying Hayden's big mouth. He said suddenly, "I'd better confess about making a phone call."

The kids seated nearby became silent. Cody went on in a louder voice, "The call I made was to Channel Two's news hotline to tell them Houston has a new bus. It's called the Hayden. It used to run on gas from eating too many burritos, but it was polluting the city, so now it runs on hot air. The news people told me I had the wrong channel. Anything that concerns Hayden belongs on Animal Planet."

A couple of people laughed. Eddie tried to smother a giggle as Hayden scowled.

"Let's get out of here," Hayden snapped. He got up from the table. "C'mon guys."

Brad and Eddie did as he ordered, and Brad managed to give Cody a shove, knocking him off the end of the bench.

Cody picked himself up from the floor. He took his tray to the clean-up window at the other end of the cafeteria and left. He wished he could escape the looks and whispers and sit quietly in the sheltered stairway outside the building, but he couldn't. He realized that it was more important than ever that he stay in sight of the kids in the school, as Jake had told him to do.

Cody sat in the library, in full view of anybody in the hall passing the floor-to-ceiling glass walls, and opened a book. He pretended to read but started to make up jokes about Hayden.

He's so stupid that he thought he had to study to pass a blood test.

He's such a jerk, when he heard people talking about the terrible Midwest tornadoes, he thought they meant a football team.

Someone pulled out the chair next to him and sat down. The person chuckled and said, "I heard what you told your cousin. That was pretty good."

Cody turned in surprise to see a guy he knew only as

Bobby, who usually needed a haircut and who mostly kept to himself. "I also heard that you made a phone call yesterday and set off a bomb scare," Bobby said.

"I didn't!"

Bobby shrugged. "They think you did. Wish I'd been here to see all the excitement. Police came and everything. Right?" He gave a loud sniff and rubbed his dripping nose with the back of one hand.

Cody glared at Bobby. "I don't want to talk about it."

"How come?"

"Because I don't like being blamed for something I didn't do."

Bobby grinned.

Angry now, Cody snapped, "You said you weren't here. Why weren't you?"

"Bad cold." Bobby wiped his nose on his hand again.

"Well, then, you could have made the call easier than me," Cody said.

Bobby didn't answer. He just kept smiling.

Cody stood, sweeping up his books. There was no way he was going to let Bobby taunt him. Fortunately, the bell rang, and Cody headed for his next class.

Eagerly, he kept looking for Jake to appear. He'd be visiting the school each day, and Cody was counting on seeing his friendly smile.

It wasn't until Cody was passing Ms. Jackson's room later, on his way to P.E., that he heard Jake's deep laugh. Cody stopped, backed up two steps, and glanced through the open doorway. He saw Jake leaning against Ms. Jackson's desk, apparently sharing a joke with her, because both of them were smiling.

Quickly, before either of them could notice him, Cody hurried on toward the gym. *Why'd Jake go to see her?* Cody thought resentfully. Ms. Jackson was nice enough, he supposed, but she was a teacher. He felt as if his friend had gone over to the enemy. He'd expected Jake to come talk to him.

There was no sign of Hayden and his buddies as Cody reluctantly trudged home after school. He hesitated on the sidewalk between his grandmother's house and the Nortons'. His mother had made it clear that he was expected there, and he didn't have a choice. His mother just didn't understand about Hayden.

For that matter, Cody didn't understand Hayden. Jake had said that bullies had a reason for being bullies. He had also said that perps had a reason for being perps. What reason did Hayden have for being so mean and trying to get all the kids to think that Cody had made that phone call? What was Hayden's problem? As Jake would ask, what was his motive?

The front door to Hayden's house opened, and Rosalie Norton stepped out on the small porch. "There you are, Cody," she said. "Hayden has been home for at least fifteen minutes. I was beginning to worry about you."

As Cody walked toward her, she kept talking. "I've got a committee meeting to attend in just half an hour, and it's not far—the Junior League building—but I want to make sure that you're settled at the dining room table with your homework before I leave. Alma's been baking some Mexican wedding cookies. They're buttery and full of chopped pecans, rolled in powdered sugar as soon as they're baked. You'll like them; Hayden does."

As they walked into the dining room, Hayden looked up from where he was seated, his books in front of him, and smirked at Cody.

Cody put his books on the table, as far away from Hayden as he could get, pulled out one of the carved mahogany chairs, and sat down.

"You better get started on your *Hamlet* project," Hayden said. "It's due in two days."

Cody shrugged. "Is yours done already? It only has to be two pages. That won't take long."

"It will if you don't have any ideas. I bet you haven't thought of an idea yet."

Cody frowned at Hayden. "I do have an idea," he said, and opened his notebook.

"Bet you don't."

"Now, Hayden," Mrs. Norton said. "Cody's a fine student and highly responsible about getting his homework done on time. You could use him as an example."

Cody tried to ignore Hayden's scowl and studied the first suggestion on Ms. Jackson's list, which he had copied from the board. His mom had said to get along with Hayden. Okay. He'd try. He said to Hayden, "I'm writing about the last scene, in which Hamlet finally does what his father's ghost asked him to do and avenges his father's murder."

Alma came to the door of the dining room and greeted Cody, then said to Mrs. Norton, "My powdered sugar is gone. I've looked everywhere for it, and I can't find it."

"Maybe we're out of it," Mrs. Norton said.

"No. We have a new bag—the large, two-pound size. It was on the list with my last shopping order. I remember unpacking the grocery sacks as soon as they were delivered. I put the powdered sugar away myself on the top shelf of the pantry, where I always keep it."

"Oh, dear. I'm sorry but I haven't got time to help you look for it now," Mrs. Norton said. "Bye, boys." She followed Alma into the kitchen, and soon Cody heard the back door shut and his aunt's car move down the driveway.

He wished his aunt had stayed home. At least Alma was here. Hayden wouldn't try something in front of Alma. Cody knew his best defense against Hayden was to stay right where he was, where Alma could see and hear him. He'd work on his *Hamlet* project, now that he'd decided what it was going to be.

But he couldn't concentrate. He couldn't stop thinking about what Bobby had said.

Bobby had admitted that he hadn't been at school the day before. That meant he would have been free to make the call from the pay phone. He seemed to think it was funny that Hayden, Brad, and Eddie had tried to make everybody blame Cody. He wouldn't think that was funny unless he knew how wrong it was. Had Bobby made that call? It hadn't occurred to Cody until this second that it could have been someone who was not in school that day.

There was a knock at the back door, and Cody could hear Alma talking to someone. In a few minutes she came into the dining room and said, "Hayden, Brad and Eddie are here to see you."

Hayden said to Alma, "Tell them to wait for me in the clubhouse. I'm almost through with this chapter." But he didn't look at Alma. He stared at Cody.

Alma left, and Hayden said to Cody, "*You* stay out. Understand?" and he walked out.

Cody didn't answer. He just stared back. He didn't want to go with them into their dumb old clubhouse.

He heard Alma say in the kitchen, "Hayden, did you bring down your pants with the torn pocket, like I asked you to?"

"I forgot," Hayden said.

"Then if you'd please run upstairs and get them for me, I'd—"

"Sorry," he called, and the back door banged shut.

Alma's heels clicked across the floor as she walked through the kitchen and into the dining room, muttering under her breath. But she stopped as she glanced at Cody.

"Cody," she said, "I've got to keep an eye on the cookies I've got in the oven. Would you mind running upstairs to Hayden's bedroom? It's the first room on the right. There's a pair of those khaki pants you boys wear to school. You'll probably find them on the floor or thrown over a chair. They've got a tear in the right pocket. Would you get them for me, please?"

The buzzer on the oven timer went off, and she hurried back into the kitchen without waiting for his answer.

Cody got up slowly. There was no telling what horrible thing Hayden would think of to do if he found Cody in his room. But Alma had asked him to go up there, and he couldn't refuse. Hayden was out in his clubhouse and wouldn't be likely to come back for a while.

Cody made his way to the front staircase and climbed the stairs. He opened the door of Hayden's room and walked inside.

He had expected Hayden's room to be messy, but it wasn't. He'd forgotten that Aunt Rosalie and Alma would pick up after Hayden. The bed was neatly made, and although there were piles of books, papers, and CDs on the chest of drawers and desk, they'd been pushed into orderly rows. Even the little red fish on the computer's screen saver swam in orderly lines.

There was no sign of the torn pants on the chair or floor.

Cody opened the door of the closet. There on the floor were the pants, dumped onto a pile with a couple of

Hayden's T-shirts. Cody bent down and picked up the pants, ready to search for a torn pocket. But his shoe dislodged a brown paper grocery bag that was under the pile of dirty clothing.

Cody reached down to return the bag to the spot where it had been, but its contents puzzled him. The bag felt firm but soft and pliable under his fingers.

Curious about what might be in the paper bag, he opened it. Inside, he found a large plastic two-pound sack of powdered sugar.

It must be the sugar Alma had said was missing from the kitchen. Why would it be hidden on the floor of Hayden's closet? Powdered sugar? It made no sense.

Suddenly Cody heard footsteps outside the door and Eddie's voice asking, "You've got it up here?"

Dropping the pants and T-shirts back on top of the paper bag, Cody dove into Hayden's closet and shut the door. He squirmed as far back behind the clothing as he could go, desperately hoping he was well hidden.

He heard Hayden answer right outside the closet door. "I couldn't sneak it out to the clubhouse. This seemed like the best place to hide it at the moment."

As the closet door opened, Cody's heart banged so loudly he was afraid Hayden would be able to hear it. He closed his eyes.

CHAPTER EIGHT

Cody heard the rustle of paper as the bag was picked up. The door closed with a snap, and he leaned back against the wall, weak and shaken.

He heard Eddie say, "This ought to do it. They'll think it's him."

"It was lucky for us he disappeared during lunch period. That made it easy," Brad said. He giggled and added, "We better make sure he's still in the dining room."

"Where else would he be?" said Eddie. "We can't go through there and take the chance that Alma will see us. We'll go out through the front door, the way we came in."

Cody was surprised to hear Hayden say, "I don't know about this, guys. I'm not sure it's a good idea."

"Don't worry so much, Hayden," Eddie responded. "It's a great idea!"

As the voices moved farther away, Cody heard Hayden ask, "Are you sure you know how to make it all work?"

"Positive, I got the—"

The bedroom door shut, and the room was silent.

Cody waited a moment, making sure they had gone, before he climbed out from behind the clothing. He was breathing hard and his palms were wet. He had to lean against the wall and wait for his heart to slow down and his legs to stop wobbling before he could pick up Hayden's pants and go downstairs.

Alma met him in the dining room. "I was coming to look for you," she said. "What took you so long?"

"I—I was trying to find the pants," Cody said as he held them out to her. "They were on the floor of the closet."

"Thanks," she said, taking the pants from him. "I'll bring you some cookies as soon as they've cooled. I sprinkled a little granulated sugar on them. They're not the same as when they're rolled in powdered sugar, but they still taste good."

As though she had done it a thousand times, Alma quickly turned the pants' pockets inside out and removed two quarters, a pack of chewing gum, and a scrap of paper. She glanced at the paper and tossed it, with the gum and coins, on the table.

The paper lay in front of Cody, faceup. He couldn't help seeing that the only thing written on it was a phone number—starting with the local area code, 713, followed by 555. The last four numbers—4321, like a countdown—were odd enough to remember.

Cody smiled at Alma and forced himself to go back to the table and face the list of topics. What could he say about Hamlet's decision to avenge his father?

When he thought of the word *father,* he realized again how much he missed his own. Suddenly he had an idea.

Ladies and gentlemen of the jury, by interrogating the members of the court who are still left standing—who, I must admit, aren't many—I have been able to prove to you that Hamlet was not in his right mind. In fact, we might say that he was one Danish short of a complete breakfast. He had the chance to keep on being Prince of Denmark, but he really blew it. Because of a murderous uncle, a dishonest mother, and a ghostly father, he—

"Here's a plate of cookies and a glass of milk for you," Alma said, so close to Cody's ear that he jumped.

It wasn't until after dinner that Cody had a chance to visit with his grandmother.

"I told you I'd help you with the paper you need to write about *Hamlet,*" she reminded him.

He helped fluff up her pillows and asked, "Do you feel like it, Grandma? Are you sure you aren't too tired?"

"As a matter of fact, I feel much better," she said. "I think this new medication is just what I needed. I helped Hayden with his theme, and now it's your turn."

Cody looked at her in surprise. "When was Hayden here?"

"We did our work over the telephone," she answered. "Hayden called while you were helping clean the kitchen. Now, what's your topic?"

"How Hamlet avenges his father's murder in the last scene of the play."

"Oh, dear," Mrs. Norton said. "I think you'd better pick another topic. That's the one Hayden chose. I can't give you both the same advice."

Cody swallowed what he wanted to say. Hayden had asked what his idea was and then had used it. He should have expected Hayden to do something mean like that. Cody thought fast.

"Grandma," Cody said, "I'd like to write about Hamlet's state of mind—whether he was just pretending to be crazy or really was. But everybody has a different opinion. Nobody is sure."

"Then write about the various possibilities," she said. "It's an interesting idea."

Cody sighed. "Okay, if you help me, Grandma," he said.

"Of course I will," she answered. "Get your notebook and pen, and we'll get busy."

The next morning, when Cody's alarm clock sounded, he woke up feeling pretty good. Maybe, he thought, it was because his *Hamlet* project had been written and was no longer on his mind. With his grandmother's help, his report was okay. Well, maybe more than okay. In fact, it was good. He was counting on getting a good grade.

Before leaving for school, he put the report inside the top drawer of his dresser for safekeeping. He arrived at school with just enough time to dump some books in his locker and get to his first class before the bell rang. Down the hall he noticed Bobby ambling into one of the science rooms. He wondered again if Bobby had made the threatening phone call.

Jake had said that most calls like that were simply pranks by people who were bored, or were carrying a grudge, or just didn't think about right and wrong. Did that fit Bobby? It wasn't any secret that Bobby barely made it from one grade to the next. Would that make him bored or angry enough to threaten the school? And was it just a threat? Or would he do something about it?

Cody shook himself and settled down at his desk. The whole thing was over, there hadn't been a second phone call, and he wasn't going to waste any more time thinking about it. He wasn't thinking about anything that had happened the day before, either. That Hayden—wouldn't it be great if he could really tell his mother and grandmother the truth?

At lunch period, as Cody stopped off at his locker, Hayden shoved him so hard he slammed against the wall, dropping his books.

"Cut it out!" Cody yelled.

He bent to pick up his books, but Brad kicked one of them out of his reach. Eddie scooped up Cody's notebook. "Got your *Hamlet* paper in here?" he asked.

"No, I haven't!" Cody tried to reach for his notebook, but Hayden got in the way.

"Betcha haven't even written it yet," Brad taunted.

"None of your business."

Hayden grinned at Cody and said, "Nobody cares, cousin. Don't sweat it." He took the notebook from Eddie and shoved it hard into Cody's stomach.

Cody grabbed it and watched the Triple Trouble saunter down the hall in the direction of the cafeteria. Quickly he retrieved his books and stuffed everything into his locker. The hallway was emptying fast, and he needed to catch up with the others and be seen in the cafeteria.

Twice Cody saw Hayden turn to look at him. Then from the corner of his eye, he caught the movement of someone going in the opposite direction. He turned and noticed Bobby opening a door and slipping through, shutting it behind him.

Cody knew that it was the door to the school's basement. It had a large KEEP OUT sign posted on it, and only the janitors were allowed to open it.

Bobby didn't belong in there with all the machinery that kept the heaters and air conditioners and water supply and electrical units going. Cody had to find out what Bobby was up to. He jogged to the door, opened it, and followed Bobby's path.

Cement steps led down to a large, deep basement, which was lit with bright exposed lightbulbs. Ahead of Cody, as he walked down the stairs, were large machines that hummed and rattled and purred and even hissed. There were passageways between them, and Cody walked through one of them. With the noise from the machinery, no one could hear his footsteps, but he couldn't hear Bobby's, either. As he passed the last of the machines, he found himself facing a small, square room with an open door. Inside were a desk, a chair, and a few old file cabinets. The room was empty, so where was Bobby? How could he just disappear?

Cody was ready to retrace his steps when he realized there was another door, partially hidden behind a battered old screen. Hesitantly, he took hold of the doorknob and slowly turned it, pulling on the door.

It opened to the outside. Cody walked up a flight of cement steps and emerged on the side street next to the school. Could this be the way Bobby had gone? Cody hadn't been that far behind him. Surely, he should have been able to see him somewhere on the block.

But Cody realized that Bobby had seemed to know where he was going, as though he'd used this route before. Cody, in contrast, had been slow and cautious in following him. A couple of minutes' difference would have made it easy for Bobby to disappear from sight.

Cody descended the steps and reached out to open the door to the janitors' office. He tugged, but the knob wouldn't turn in his hand. Apparently, the door had locked automatically, and he wouldn't be able to get back in.

He had no choice but to walk around the block to either the front doors or the yard in back. Cody groaned as he realized he'd probably have some explaining to do. He just hoped it wouldn't be to Coach Anderson.

Cody saw her at the same time she spied him. Standing by the wire fence that surrounded the schoolyard, Coach Anderson spotted Cody, started with surprise, and went to meet him at the gate.

"What were you doing off campus?" she demanded.

Cody had his mouth open, ready to explain, when the school's loud alarm went off.

Coach Anderson swung open the gate with one hand and grabbed Cody's arm with the other. Making sure the gate was locked, she marched Cody across the yard toward the students who were hurrying to line up.

"If that's another bomb threat, you're in big trouble!" she yelled into Cody's ear.

He winced and stumbled, trying to keep up with her long strides. He was in trouble, all right. There was no doubt about it.

CHAPTER NINE

There had been a second threatening telephone call to the school. The caller's voice had been muffled, so some of his words were indistinct, but Mr. Carmody insisted that it was the same voice he had heard the first time.

"He said 'smoke,' " Mr. Carmody reported. "I know I heard him say 'smoke.' "

Cody, who'd been detained after all the other kids had been allowed to go home early, faced Mr. Carmody, Mrs. Allen, the school's short, plump secretary, Coach Anderson, and Jake, who had responded to the police call.

"I didn't do it," Cody began.

"That's what you said last time," Coach Anderson snapped. "Do we need to get his mother in here?"

"I didn't do it then, either."

"Why don't you tell us what you *did* do?" Jake broke in. "Tell us where you were and why."

Cody left out the part about the hassle with Hayden. He just said that he had seen Bobby open the door into the basement and go inside, and he had followed.

"I don't think it could have been Bobby," Mrs. Allen

interrupted. "Just before lunch he came into the office with a headache and said his cold was worse. I sent him to the nurse's office to rest and called his mother. She was at her office, but she said she'd come by as soon as she could to pick him up."

"Did she?" Jake asked.

"I don't know. Right after that I went to the teachers' lounge."

"It *was* Bobby," Cody insisted. "I saw him."

"Okay, Cody," Jake said. "Just give us your story. Tell us the rest."

"There isn't anything much left to tell," Cody said. "I walked through that big room with all the machinery and found a small room way at the end with a desk in it."

"Did you see Bobby while you were down there?" Mr. Carmody asked.

"No. I didn't see him at all. But there was another door, and I opened it. It led outside, so I went up the steps to see if Bobby had gone out that way."

Before anyone could ask, Cody quickly added, "I didn't see him, so I went back down the stairs. Only the door had shut and locked itself, and I had to come around the block to get back into the school."

Coach Anderson interrupted, "And that's where I saw Cody."

Mr. Carmody scowled at Cody. "You're trying to tell us you followed a boy who was reported to be in the nurse's office?"

"He wasn't in the nurse's office when I saw him." Cody felt a tear slide down his cheek, and he rubbed at his face. The situation he was in looked hopeless, but he was too old to break down and cry.

"We need to talk to the nurse," Jake said. "She can verify whether Bobby was in her office. She was in the teachers' lounge eating lunch with me when the alarm went off."

Jake turned to Mr. Carmody. "Was Bobby out here with the other students after the alarm sounded?"

"The school was cleared of all personnel," Mr. Carmody insisted.

"I didn't ask that," Jake said. "I asked if anyone saw Bobby in the schoolyard with the other students."

For an instant there was silence.

"Before I leave, I'll get Bobby's home address and phone number from you," Jake told Mrs. Allen. "And, of course, we'll check the source of the phone call, as we did before."

Indignantly, Coach Anderson asked, "What are you going to do about Cody Carter?"

"Nothing," Jake said.

"B-but he's a s-suspect!" she stammered.

"He told us where he was and why he was there," Jake said. "There's no evidence to prove that he was anywhere else."

Mr. Carmody pursed his lips as he thought. "He was not supposed to be down in the basement. There is a clearly marked KEEP OUT sign posted on the door. I'm afraid Cody will have to serve a Saturday detention."

Coach Anderson nodded agreement and looked partially satisfied.

"So be it," Jake said. He gave Cody a quick pat on the shoulders and glanced over at a group of teachers who were standing together in a spot of shade.

Cody saw that Ms. Jackson was looking back at Jake and smiling.

"Right now I'll ask your teachers a few questions. Then I'll check with the bomb squad to see how soon y'all can get back into the building," Jake said.

Mr. Carmody looked down his nose at Cody and said, "You are dismissed."

"Yes, sir," Cody said. He cut out the side gate and headed for home.

His mother met him at the kitchen door with a finger to her lips. "Shhh. Grandma's finally been able to get to sleep," she said. Obviously, the school hadn't contacted her yet.

Cody flopped into the nearest kitchen chair and leaned on the table, propping up his chin in his hands. "The school got another bomb threat," he said.

Mrs. Carter sat next to him and put an arm around his shoulders. "That's terrible," she said. "But at least this time no one is blaming you."

Cody groaned and said, "Mom, that's not the way it was. I'll tell you everything that happened, and I want you to believe me. I didn't make that telephone call."

"I do believe you," she said, and she listened while Cody poured out the whole story.

When he finished, he said, "Jake is going to check where the phone call came from, and he's going to talk to Bobby and his mom and see what he can find out."

It suddenly occurred to Cody that his mom hadn't been surprised when he told her about the phone call. "You already knew about the call," he said. "Did someone from the school telephone you?"

Mrs. Carter shook her head. "No. Hayden and his friends told me. I asked why they were out of school early."

"Hayden was here?"

"Yes. He and the other boys visited for a while with Grandma. That's why she's sleeping now. She loves to have visitors, but they tire her."

Cody stiffened as the jealous ache returned. *She's* my

grandma! he wanted to shout, as if he were a little kid. But, of course, she was Hayden's grandmother, too.

Mrs. Carter suddenly enveloped Cody in a smothering hug. "Oh, honey, don't look so unhappy. Grandma is going to get better. I promise. And Aunt Tillie is thinking about selling her house in Arkansas and moving in with Grandma so neither one of them will be alone—maybe by Christmas."

Feeling guilty because his mother had the wrong idea about what was disturbing him, Cody pulled away. He tried to sort through what she had said. "Do you mean your aunt Tillie will live with us, too?"

"We'll make sure that Tillie is settled in and Grandma is feeling well and both of them are happy with the arrangement. Then we'll be able to go home. Of course," Mrs. Carter said, "that means we have to do our best to help Grandma get well. I know that you and Hayden will cooperate."

Cody sighed. Why did adults say they knew something when they couldn't possibly know it? "When the guys were here, what else did they tell you?" he asked.

"Eddie said something about seeing you follow that boy you mentioned, Bobby, but Hayden pulled him out of the kitchen, so I didn't hear the rest."

Mrs. Carter smiled at Cody. "But you told me the whole story. I didn't need to hear it from Eddie."

"The principal and the coach still think I made the calls, Mom."

She patted his shoulder. "We both know you didn't. Sooner or later the real culprit will turn up and the case will be solved."

Cody remembered what Jake had said about the perps who made these calls. They weren't always found out. It wasn't that easy.

His thoughts took a sudden turn. "Mom," he asked, "what would you do with a two-pound sack of powdered sugar?"

"A sack that big would last a good long time in our house," she said. "Powdered sugar is good sprinkled on cinnamon toast and dusted on brownies. And I suppose, with that much on hand, I'd find plenty of cookie recipes that would call for it."

"Would you only use it for cooking?"

"I can't think of anything else powdered sugar would be used for." She looked at the clock. "Hadn't you better get to your homework?"

"I can't," he said. "My books are all in my locker, and we couldn't get into the building because the bomb squad had to examine it."

"Well, whatever you decide to do, be quiet about it," she told him. "We don't want to disturb Grandma's nap."

"I'll do some stuff on my computer," Cody said. He walked upstairs wondering why he hadn't thought of a computer search before. Hayden and the other guys weren't going to use that powdered sugar in cooking. They had something else in mind. Maybe a search engine like Google could tell him what that might be.

He watched as the screen brought up sites with recipes that called for powdered sugar. Only one site differed from the rest. Powdered sugar helped fight mites that infected bees. Hayden, Brad, and Eddie weren't planning to help bees. Cody was sure of that.

He remembered that the telephone caller had used the word *smoke,* so he typed it into the Search box and hit Enter.

He saw Web sites for antismoking campaigns, smoke detectors, and cigar stores. He stopped when he found a Web site devoted to smoke and bees.

Powdered sugar and bees, smoke and bees? Was there a connection? Cody sighed. If there was, he couldn't figure it out.

Puzzled, Cody shut down his computer, flopped across his bed, and tried to think. Instead, he fell asleep.

He woke to find his mother gently shaking his shoulder. "Office Ramsey is here to talk to you," she said.

Cody jumped to his feet so fast he staggered, bouncing off the dresser and desk on the way to his open bedroom door. He hurried down the stairs, trying not to make too much noise, and dashed into the living room.

Not even taking time to say hello to Jake, Cody asked, "Did Bobby confess?"

"Slow down," Jake said. He patted the sofa cushion next to his. "Have a seat and I'll fill you in on what we found out."

Cody immediately sat down, aware that his mother had taken the easy chair near the fireplace. "What was it?" he asked in a rush.

"Bobby left the school just as you said, through the basement door. His mom had already arrived at the school and was waiting for him at the side street, where she had picked him up before."

Cody scowled, trying to think. "Why didn't he go out the front doors, the regular way?"

"He claimed he didn't like having a lot of kids and Mr. Carmody watch him leave. He'd used the door before, and his mom had picked him up there before."

Cody looked up. "How about the phone call?"

"It came from the same place as the first one. Outside the convenience store."

"I suppose Bobby and his mom didn't stop at that store." Cody slumped, waiting for the answer he knew would come.

"They say they didn't," Jake told him. "They went straight home."

"Didn't anybody see the person making the phone call?"

"The people at the convenience store claimed they couldn't. As I told you before, the public telephone is located outside, out of sight of the checkout counter."

"We're back where we started," Cody said.

"Not completely," Jake answered. "We know that the calls were made when you were away from the other kids, with no one to alibi you. Once could be coincidence. Twice makes me begin to think someone planned it that way."

Cody sat upright. "You mean I was set up?"

"I didn't say for sure," Jake cautioned him. "I just said it was a possibility."

"Hayden," Cody said.

His mother leaned forward. "Cody, Hayden is your cousin. You're imagining things he might do to you. Your last complaint about him was that he planned to shove your head in a toilet."

"Mom, he *said* he would."

"Did he do it?"

Cody squirmed. "Well, no, but—"

"See what I mean?" Mrs. Carter said. "Hayden wouldn't harm you or make threatening phone calls and try to get people to think you made them. Give Hayden a chance to be your friend, and he will be. Please don't let me hear you say one more word about suspecting Hayden of anything."

Jake was more direct. He said to Cody, "Do you know for a fact that Hayden saw you go outside to eat lunch or go into the basement?"

"I saw him in the hall, going to the cafeteria, so he might have."

"I didn't ask if he might have seen you. I asked if you knew for a fact."

Cody closed his eyes, trying as hard as he could to remember. Finally, he opened them and shook his head. "No," he said. "I'm not sure where Hayden was."

"Do you see how silly it is to blame Hayden for everything?" she asked. "It wasn't you, but it's not Hayden."

Jake didn't give Cody a chance to answer. "Keep thinking about what you heard and saw," he said. "Something might occur to you."

"What can you do with a two-pound bag of powdered sugar?" Cody asked.

Jake smiled. "I give up. What?"

"No, this is not a joke. I really need to know."

Jake cocked his head and studied Cody. "Why?"

Cody quickly glanced at his mother. After what she had said, there was no way he could bring up Hayden.

He shrugged. "I don't know. I was just wondering."

Jake said, "First of all, you can cook with it."

"That's what I told him," Mrs. Carter said.

"And it's possible to . . ." Jake stopped, thought a moment, and got to his feet. "I'll have to think on it a minute." Then, as if he were deliberately changing the subject, he said, "By the way, you might like to know that I got a spot on the open-mike schedule at the club for tomorrow night. I've worked out a routine about Texas, and I'm using the joke about Texas I bought from you. The musicians in my group actually laughed at it, so I'm hoping the audience will, too. There's nothing rougher to face than a dead audience. Every stand-up comic hopes and prays that the audience will be with him."

"What if it isn't?"

"Then you work to win it over. It's sort of like what an attorney has to do to win over a jury."

"Could I go to the club and hear you?" Cody asked.

Jake shook his head. "I wish you could. I know I can count on you to laugh at my jokes. But you're too young to go to a club, Cody. I'll have to tell you all about it. Or Ms. Jackson can tell you. She told me she'd be there. Just cross your fingers for me that the audience will think I'm funny."

"What'll you do if they don't?" Cody asked.

"What other stand-ups do when the people in an audience sit on their hands—pretend that they're laughing and applauding, and keep going, giving it the best I can."

As Cody and his mother walked to the front door with Jake, the officer said, "Wish me luck."

"We will," Cody said, but he thought, *Somebody had better wish me luck, too. If we don't find out who made those calls to the school, I'm really going to need it.*

CHAPTER TEN

Friday morning, right after breakfast, Cody opened his top dresser drawer and reached inside to get his *Hamlet* report. As he stared inside the drawer, filled with nothing but rolled-up socks, he felt his mouth drop open in shock. The report he had put in the drawer for safekeeping wasn't there.

He tugged open the other drawers, slamming them as he saw they didn't hold his report, either. "Mom!" he wailed.

His mother, who had come upstairs at the same time he had, appeared in an instant. The clean sheets she had taken from the linen closet were piled in her hands. "What in the world is the matter?" she asked.

"My *Hamlet* report!" Cody answered. "It was right here in the top drawer, and now it's gone!"

"It has to be somewhere," she said. "Can you remember where you put it?"

"I know where I put it!" Cody said. He glanced at the clock. In less than twenty minutes he'd have to leave for school. Where was his report?

He and his mother searched the room, even checking under the bed. The paper he had so painstakingly written was nowhere in sight.

Cody dropped onto his bed as a horrible thought hit him. "Mom," he said, "when Hayden, Brad, and Eddie were here yesterday afternoon, did you let any of them come up here into my room?"

"Honey, I was working in the kitchen, cutting up carrots and potatoes for the stew. I didn't check to see where the boys were."

"They took my report."

"I thought we'd settled this suspicion you have about Hayden. Why do you blame him for everything? He had written his own report. Grandma helped him, we know that. He wouldn't want yours."

"He would, Mom. He'd want to take it just to get me in trouble." Cody jumped to his feet and strode toward the open doorway.

"Where are you going?" Mrs. Carter asked.

"To get my report back."

"Cody!" He wobbled off balance as his mother clamped a hand on his shoulder. "You are absolutely not going to Hayden's house to accuse him of taking your report," Mrs. Carter said. "You have no proof that he did."

"Mom, I know he did."

"Prove it to *me*."

Cody thought a moment. Of course he had no proof. He just knew. He also knew that his mother wasn't going to buy that argument. He'd have to try another. "Maybe he's just playing a joke, trying to scare me," he suggested.

Mrs. Carter looked stern. "If it's a joke," she said, "then he'll give back your report and everything will be fine. But there will be no anger and no accusations. Nothing that will upset the family. Do you understand?"

Cody nodded, but he felt a sick knot in his stomach. "I understand," he said.

Mrs. Carter glanced at the clock. "You'd better continue to get ready for school. You don't have much time left before you have to leave."

Cody realized he must look as miserable as he felt, because his mother put an arm around his shoulders and kissed the top of his head. "Honey," she said, "I know things are difficult for you right now, but these problems will work themselves out. I promise."

"Sure, Mom," Cody said. As soon as his mother had left the room, he hurried as quietly as he could down the stairs, out the front door, and over to the Nortons' house. He rang the doorbell.

When Alma opened the door, she looked at him in surprise. "Change your mind?" she asked.

Startled, Cody asked, "About what?"

"About going to school with Hayden. He asked his dad for a ride because he had to take his English project to school, and Mr. Norton told him to call you and ask if you'd like a ride, too. So Hayden did, and you said you'd rather walk. Now they've already left." Alma rolled her eyes. "You kids can't remember things from one minute to the next."

"What's Hayden's project?" Cody asked.

"Who knows? It was in a box. He says it's a big secret."

Cody knew that Hayden had written a report based on a stolen idea. A two-page paper couldn't be heavy enough to require a lift to school. But he had no time to try to puzzle out the answer now. "Alma," he said, "I think I left part of my project in Hayden's room. Could I run up there and see if I can find it?"

"Sure," she said, glancing at her wristwatch. "But make it fast or you're going to be late."

Cody took the stairs two at a time to get to Hayden's room. He fumbled through the stack of papers on Hayden's desk and threw open the drawers, searching in vain for the *Hamlet* report he had written.

"Cody?" Alma called from the bottom of the stairs. "Did you find what you needed?"

Cody's last chance was the wastepaper basket. He looked into it and saw that it was filled with torn scraps of paper. He scooped up a handful, sick when he recognized his own handwriting. His report! There was no way he could tape the pieces back together.

"Cody?"

He had begun to let the handful of scraps fall through his fingers when the computer-printed words "powdered sugar" on one of them caught his eye. Snatching up the scrap, he read what looked like part of a recipe on it. There were a few letters that seemed to be the name of a chemical, then "Cook over low" and something else about a long waxed string.

"Cody! You better hurry or you'll get detention for being late!"

Cody shoved the scrap of paper into his pocket and dashed down the stairs. He needed to talk to Jake. But right now he'd have to run all the way to school.

Just as the first bell was ringing, Cody made it into his first-period class. He dropped into his seat, hot, sweaty, and panting for breath.

Hayden, Eddie, and Brad, turned and grinned at him.

The map his history teacher was unrolling slipped from his hands with a bang, and Cody jumped back into the present. There was no way he'd have time to rewrite his report before English class, but he had to come up with something.

Ms. Jackson had said she wanted them to use their

own original ideas. Okay. What he'd just been thinking might work. If he did what Jake said a detective had to do, then he might be able to save himself.

Cody patted his back pocket, checking for his wallet. Yep. It was there. And inside it was the business card Jake had given him. As soon as he could manage it, he was going to talk to Jake.

CHAPTER ELEVEN

Cody was able to avoid Hayden, Brad, and Eddie until English class, but he saw each of them carry his written report up to Ms. Jackson's desk and put it on the pile. Almost everyone in the class had chosen to write a report. But Paul, the artist, had made a poster of the final act of the play. It had cut-paper bodies and lots of painted red blood. Only Hamlet's friend Horatio had been left standing. Paul had even added a few glass eyeballs into the carnage. Cody thought it looked cool and creative.

Emily and Jennifer had created a diorama in a shoe box. A small doll, dressed as Ophelia, floated down a blue crepe-paper river, flowers in her hair. Alison, another girl who never talked in class, had cross-stitched a small, lumpy pillow with Polonius's advice to his son Laertes: "This above all, to thine own self be true."

Ms. Jackson seemed pleased with all the projects, and she smiled at the class. "Has everyone turned in a project?" she asked.

Cody was aware that Hayden was looking at him. He was sure he heard Eddie giggle. Cody held his hand high and said, "I haven't, Ms. Jackson."

She looked surprised. "Why is that, Cody?"

"Mine is an oral report. I will be conducting a trial. I'd like the class, as members of a jury, to decide whether Hamlet was sane enough to be brought to trial for the murders of Claudius and Polonius—or if he was too mentally unstable to know what he was doing."

"I like your idea of a trial, Cody. Quite original. Come up and you can get started. Have you prepared your witnesses?"

"Oh, no," Cody said as he walked to the front of the room. "I don't want to get charged with leading a witness. We're after the truth. The witnesses don't know they'll be called on to testify."

Ms. Jackson smiled. "All right," she said. "I'll turn the classroom over to you. Court is in session. Begin, please."

Cody tried to stand as tall as he could and looked over his audience, who stared back. For a moment he wished he could just bolt out of the room. He realized what Jake meant by a dead audience, but he remembered what Jake said a detective had to do.

He even thought of his father's skills as an attorney. He gathered his courage, took a deep breath, and turned the chair kept for classroom visitors so that it faced the class. He began, "I'd like Jennifer, lady-in-waiting to Queen Gertrude, to take the stand."

Jennifer frowned and didn't budge.

Before anyone could say anything, Ms. Jackson piped up. "By the way, everyone who cooperates by taking the part of a witness will get extra credit."

"How much credit?" Jennifer asked.

"Five points."

Jennifer slid out of her seat, walked to the empty chair, sat down, and waited.

"Are you Jennifer, attendant to Queen Gertrude of Denmark?" Cody asked her.

Jennifer looked scornful. "If you say so."

"You were with her a lot. Did she ever talk to you about her son, Prince Hamlet?"

"Yes."

"Was she worried about him?"

"Yes."

"Why?"

Jennifer squirmed in her chair. Then she answered, "Okay, Gertrude wanted Hamlet to stop moping around because his father had died and also to stop acting so angry with her." It almost seemed to Cody that Jennifer was getting into the role.

"Did she know why he was angry with her?" he continued.

"She knew he didn't like the fact that she had married Claudius so soon, but don't blame Gertrude for that," Jennifer said defensively. "Think about what life was like for women at that time. She was a queen, and by marrying Claudius she could go on being a queen. If she didn't marry him, then what was she supposed to do? What was a queen to do? Take a job serving as a waitress in a tavern or scrubbing floors?"

"The witness is getting off the subject," Cody remarked. To Jennifer he said, "Did she believe Polonius when he thought Hamlet was mad with love for Ophelia?"

"Well, I think she wanted to believe," Jennifer said.

"She liked Ophelia and would probably have been glad to have her as a daughter-in-law. And being mad with love was a lot better than just being mad, period."

"Let's get the facts here. Later—after Hamlet heard someone behind the curtain and stabbed him—did she change her mind?" Cody asked.

"Well, sure," Jennifer answered. "As she told King Claudius, Hamlet yelled, 'A rat! A rat!' and stabbed Polonius through the curtain."

"Would you say that Hamlet's own mother thought he was crazy?"

Jennifer thought for only a moment. "Yes," she said with certainty.

"Thank you for your testimony," Cody told her. "You may step down."

As Jennifer went back to her seat, Cody announced, "My next witness will be Emily, best friend of Ophelia."

Emily giggled, jumped from her seat, and hurried to take the witness chair. Cody noticed that most of the kids were looking interested. Paul and a guy named Bruce tried to catch his eye and pointed to themselves.

As soon as Emily was seated, Cody said, "I understand that you grew up with Ophelia, that you were friends since you were small children."

Giggling again, Emily said, "That's right."

Cody said, "Polonius showed King Claudius and Queen Gertrude some letters and poetry that Hamlet had written to Ophelia. Had she ever shown them to you?"

"The letters?" asked Emily. "Well, I'm not sure."

"Did Ophelia encourage Hamlet?" Cody asked pointedly.

Emily broke off midgiggle and said, "I guess not

really. I mean, her father thought Hamlet wasn't really planning to marry Ophelia because he would someday be King of Denmark and he'd have to marry somebody of royal birth. So Polonius told her to give back his letters and poems and tell him she wouldn't see him anymore."

"Did she?" Cody pressed on.

"Yes. She did whatever her father told her to do."

"What did Hamlet do about it? Tell us as much as you know, please."

"He came to see Ophelia," Emily said. "His clothes were all messed up, and he was acting weird and saying all sorts of crazy stuff."

"Did Ophelia tell her father?"

"Yes, she did. That wasn't wrong. It wasn't tattling."

"What did he say?"

"He thought Hamlet had gone nuts because his love was rejected."

"Did Ophelia think so, too?"

"I guess she thought whatever her father wanted her to think," Jennifer answered. "At that time a girl had no choice, you know."

"So she thought he was crazy?"

"Yes."

"Thank you," Cody said. "You may be excused. I call on Hayden, attendant to King Claudius, as my next witness."

Emily, still giggling, hurried back to her seat. Hayden clutched the edge of his desk and looked at Eddie, then Brad, as if waiting for a sign as to what he should do.

Ms. Jackson said, "Hayden?"

Hayden jumped and scuttled to the chair. He wiggled his shoes and looked down, not facing Cody.

"Hayden, you served as attendant to King Claudius. Right?"

"I guess," Hayden mumbled.

Cody went on, "Doesn't that mean you helped care for his clothing, tasted his meals to make sure they weren't poisoned, cleaned his boots, and each morning emptied the pot under his bed?"

Some of the kids in the class laughed, and Hayden's face grew red. "How come you made me a servant? I might have been a knight or something."

"It's too late for wishful thinking," Cody said.

Again there was laughter, which made Cody feel good. He understood what Jake meant about seeing an audience warm up. Things were a lot better than they had been before.

"Did you provide Claudius with wine when he asked for it?"

Hayden scowled, but he answered, "Yes. I guess."

"And poison to put in the wine?"

"Don't blame me. I just did what I was told."

"Let's get this right. Are you saying that it doesn't bother you to get someone in trouble as long as someone else tells you to do it?"

Hayden glanced quickly at Eddie, then back at Cody. "Who are you talking about?"

"Claudius, of course," Cody said. "Weren't you there when he poured poison in the king's ear? And put poison on the tip of Laertes's sword so it would kill Prince Hamlet? And poisoned the wine that Queen Gertrude accidentally drank? And more recently, tore up that report in the wastebasket?"

"That wasn't me," Hayden shouted. He looked at Eddie.

Ms. Jackson looked puzzled. "Cody, I seem to be missing something here."

"Sorry," Cody said. "I'll strike that last question

from the record." Quickly he turned back to Hayden and asked, "Since you had to be on hand to do whatever Claudius asked of you, did you ever overhear any of his conversations with the queen?"

"What do you mean?" Hayden asked suspiciously.

"Did you ever hear Claudius tell Gertrude that he thought Prince Hamlet was pretending to be crazy?"

Hayden thought a minute. Cody wondered if he was trying to remember what was in the play. Finally, Hayden said, "Yeah, I heard him tell her that."

"Does that mean you can testify that Claudius thought Hamlet was putting on an act?"

"Yeah," Hayden said.

"Did you ever hear Gertrude tell him that sometimes you can go too far trying to get someone in trouble and they'll smoke you out and you're likely to get caught?"

"Smoke?" Hayden half rose from his chair.

"Just answer. Yes or no."

"Yeah. I mean no. I don't think that was in the play. Was it?" He glared at Cody.

"Thank you," Cody said. "You may return to your seat. I now call Sir Paul, cousin of Horatio."

As Hayden stumbled from the chair, Ms. Jackson said, "Good job, Hayden. I like the way you acted so nervous—just the way a reluctant witness might behave."

Cody watched Hayden hurry to his seat. Now Cody believed Eddie was the real ringleader and Hayden was just going along. One thing puzzled Cody, though—Hayden's strange reaction when Cody said "smoke you out." What was going on with the sugar and the lie that morning about bringing a big project to school?

Paul took the witness chair, and Cody brought his mind back to the business at hand. "Sir Paul, as cousin to Horatio, you know that Hamlet and Horatio were close friends. Is that right?"

"Right," Paul said. He looked as if he was enjoying himself.

"Where was Horatio when Hamlet died?"

"There with Hamlet."

"Did Hamlet give Horatio any famous last words?"

Paul nodded. "Hamlet told Horatio to stay alive so he could tell the story of what had happened."

"Did Horatio do that?"

"Did he ever," Paul said. "He talked about it all the time, even when he grew to be an old man. Frankly, some of us got sick of hearing about it."

Paul and Cody grinned at each other, and some of the kids laughed.

Cody asked, "Sir Paul, did Horatio ever say whether he thought that Hamlet was out of his mind or knew what he was doing?"

Paul looked solemn and answered, "Horatio knew that Hamlet had obeyed his father's ghost and had taken vengeance on Claudius."

"So he thought Hamlet was sane?"

"Sure," Paul said. "Remember, Horatio had seen the ghost, too. He's the one who told Hamlet his father's ghost was looking for him. Besides, Hamlet had warned Horatio that he'd probably act strange."

"Thank you," Cody said. "You may be excused."

As Paul returned to his seat, Cody faced the classroom. "Ladies and gentlemen of the jury," he said, "you have heard the evidence of our witnesses, and you have read the play.

"Now I'm going to ask you to vote, based on what you believe. How many of you think Hamlet was out of his mind and not totally responsible for what he did?"

A few hands went up, and Cody counted them.

"How many think that Hamlet, despite the weird way he sometimes acted, knew what he was doing and deliberately followed his father's wishes when he murdered Claudius?"

Most of the hands were raised, some of them waving wildly.

Cody said, "The majority has voted that Hamlet should be indicted. Because Hamlet didn't stick around, there can't be a trial. The only trial was in having to read the play. The only thing worse was having to see the movie, too. Thank you all for your civic participation."

"Hey, that was fun," Emily said, and Paul applauded. A few of the other kids joined in.

Ms. Jackson stood and said, "Cody, that was a great report. A-plus. And all you witnesses were terrific."

Cody beamed as he walked toward his seat, but as he passed Hayden he felt his glare and saw his mouth twist. Cody realized that Hayden was jealous. The thought surprised him.

Motive: jealousy. The words flashed into his mind. It didn't make any difference. Cody admitted to himself that he'd been jealous of Hayden, too. It was a lame motive for his cousin's behavior.

With a crackle from the wall speaker, the intercom sounded, and Mr. Carmody began to speak. "I have a short reminder before you leave your classes for lunch period. Today, immediately after school, our football team will be playing a home game with Mulberry Middle School. Our cheerleaders have been working hard on their performance, and we're hoping for a good turnout of our student body."

Emily giggled and gave a bounce in her seat. Cody turned to see Eddie's smug expression. They were up to something, Cody knew.

And that something probably included getting him into trouble.

Was there anything he could do about it?

CHAPTER TWELVE

As soon as the lunch bell rang, Cody hurried out the door and down to the office. He planned to use the school's telephone to call Jake, but there were some kids already waiting.

Mrs. Allen was announcing, "Take no longer than three minutes per call. Why so many of you forgot to tell your parents there was an after-school game is beyond me!"

Cody left the office. He'd eat lunch first, then call Jake.

Out in the hall he bumped into Paul, who was standing there with Bruce.

"Come eat with us," Paul told Cody. "I thought of something else you should have asked about Horatio. I'll tell you about it."

"Okay," Cody said, but he looked at each of them, puzzled. "How come you're waiting out here in the hall?"

Paul motioned toward the boys' bathroom. "Bruce was trying to decide if he wanted to go now so he wouldn't get pushed around by the crowd that will come this way after lunch."

Cody smiled. "He's doing a Hamlet."

"Huh?"

"You know, 'to pee or not to pee.' "

The guys cracked up, and Cody felt really good. He was beginning to be glad that Hayden had destroyed his written report. It had made him do something totally different, and maybe now everything was going to be better.

Paul finally stopped laughing. He clapped Cody on the shoulder and said, "Come on, y'all. Let's get lunch."

After school Cody still had to stand in line in the office for a few minutes while kids ahead of him used the phone. The halls emptied quickly as most of the students headed for the bleachers on the north side of the football field.

By the time Cody reached the phone, Mrs. Allen had stepped out of the office. Cody was glad. There was no way he could have kept her from overhearing his conversation with Jake.

Luckily, he got Jake on the first try. "It's me, Cody," he said. "I need your opinion. I found this scrap of paper and it's got something weird on it."

"Go ahead," Jake said.

Cody pulled the scrap of paper out of his pocket and read what was on it to Jake, beginning with the powdered sugar. "All the words aren't here," he said, "because the paper's torn."

"Where'd you get that paper?" Jake's voice was quick and sharp.

"Hayden's wastepaper basket."

"Where are you now?"

"At school. In the office."

"Why aren't you at home?"

"There's a game. Everybody's outside except me by this time. They're all in the bleachers."

"Is someone with you in the office? You get outside, too. I'll be right there."

Cody heard a click as Jake hung up the phone. Slowly, he replaced the receiver on the phone, wondering why Jake seemed so hurried and stern. He glanced at the phone and, for the first time, read the school's phone number: 713–555–4321.

Gasping as he stepped back from the counter, Cody realized that it was the number on the scrap of paper that Alma had taken from Hayden's school uniform pants.

It hadn't been Bobby who had made those two phone calls. Maybe it had been Hayden! Hayden, who both times had known that Cody was away from the cafeteria and out of sight of anyone who could vouch for his location.

Today Hayden brought something with him to school. Was it some kind of bomb? It couldn't be a real bomb! Maybe it was a smoke bomb. He had acted really weird on the witness stand when Cody had mentioned the word *smoke.*

Jake had said he'd get to the school soon. But Cody felt it was up to him to find Hayden and stop whatever he and his dirtbag friends were planning to do. He ran as fast as he could out of the office, through the back doors of the school, and toward the football field.

At the back of the bleachers he saw Eddie and Brad bent over, staring into the shadows, so he raced toward them. Hayden was nowhere in sight.

Just as Cody arrived, however, there was a loud hiss and a sizzle, and someone under the bleachers let out a scream.

It was Hayden who scrambled out, stumbling to his feet, his hair singed and the sleeve of his polo shirt on fire.

Cody was barely aware that Brad had stepped back and that Eddie had turned and run. Without a word, he charged into Hayden so hard he knocked him down into the dirt. He rolled Hayden onto his stomach, lying on top of him. He scooped up handfuls of dirt, pressing them against Hayden's scorched sleeve.

"The fire's out," he assured Hayden.

Suddenly people were everywhere. He was aware of yelling and scrabbling as the kids hurried from the bleachers. Police were herding the students away from a billowing cloud of white smoke, and firemen were dousing the smoke bomb.

Hands grabbed Cody's right arm and his collar, and he was roughly jerked up and off Hayden.

"I've got you!" Coach Anderson shouted.

Someone else held him tightly as the coach gently helped Hayden to his feet. "Are you hurt?" she asked. "What did Cody do to you?"

Hayden, streaked with dirt, his shirt burnt and torn, looked at Cody, anger and jealousy no longer in his eyes. His face twisted as if he was going to break down.

"I was on fire and he put it out. That's what he did," Hayden said.

Jake appeared next to Cody, who was suddenly released. "Suppose you tell us exactly what happened," Jake said to Hayden.

Hayden gulped twice, then managed to say, "I didn't want to do it. They thought it would be cool to set off a smoke bomb."

"They?"

Hayden looked around and then answered. "Eddie

and Brad. And when they saw Cody go off by himself, they got the idea of making the phone calls and getting people to think he did it."

"Not me! It was Hayden's idea!" Eddie's voice piped up, and Cody turned to see that another uniformed policeman had Eddie's shoulder in a firm grip.

Jake was stern. "Didn't you realize that what you were doing was a criminal act?"

Hayden ducked his head. "I did. I knew my parents would be mad, but I never figured we'd get caught. They said it wasn't a real bomb. It was just a smoke bomb. It was a tough-guy thing to do." He looked up at Jake.

"Tell me exactly what happened," Jake said.

"I thought the fuse sputtered out," Hayden began, "so I crawled under the bleachers to get it lit again. Only the smoke bomb went off and shot out some of the hot stuff. I got out of there fast, but my shirt was on fire. Cody knocked me down and put out the flames."

Two paramedics pushed through the crowd. "Anyone hurt?" one of them asked.

Hayden put a hand to his cheek and said, "My face stings."

"How about this kid?" the other paramedic said. "Looks like a spot on his arm."

Cody didn't try to sort out everything that was going on. There was an emergency room and doctors and Aunt Rosalie, who stopped talking only when Uncle Austin began lecturing Hayden about juvenile court and the hopeful probability of probation, community service, and "deferred adjudication." Cody was bandaged and cleaned up and finally ended up sitting quietly in his grandmother's kitchen with Hayden while his mother, aunt, and uncle talked in low tones in the living room.

Hayden suddenly broke the silence. "They're trying to decide how and what to tell Grandma."

"I think *we* should tell her, not them," Cody said.

Hayden's mouth twisted in misery. "She's going to get upset and be mad at me. And why would you be nice to me, anyway?"

"We're cousins and we could be friends. If we tell her the right way it will be better," Cody said.

"What's the right way?"

"We've got to go in there acting like friends and just tell her the part about the smoke bomb and maybe how we got you out, if she's got questions. We don't need to tell her all the other stuff you and those guys did."

Hayden thought a minute. "Okay. Like friends. But we're really not friends." Hayden looked miserable again. "I'm not going to have any friends after what happened."

"Like I said, we could be friends," Cody said. "Eddie and Brad aren't real friends. Why'd you stay with them?"

"They made me feel more grown-up. We had this clubhouse but I don't have a clubhouse anymore. Dad's already given orders to tear it down."

"That's rough," Cody said. "Well, how about it? Truce? For Grandma's sake?"

"Truce." The two cousins shook hands. "Thanks," Hayden said.

"Then come on."

Cody led the way to their grandmother's open bedroom door. Just before stepping in, he put an arm around Hayden's shoulders. After only a moment's hesitation, Hayden did the same to him.

"Hi, Grandma," they both said.

She was sitting up in her easy chair, propped on each side with pillows, and seemed to be feeling a lot better.

"Hi," she said. "What happened? I know there's been a commotion."

"Smoke bomb got smoky," Cody said. "It went off too soon."

Mrs. Norton looked concerned. "I know sometimes boys do dumb things," she said, "but smoke bombs are dangerous. I hope I won't hear about something like this again."

"Don't worry. You won't," Hayden said. "It was my dumb idea."

"It's nice to see you two together. How'd the *Hamlet* reports go?" she asked.

"I don't know yet," Hayden said. "The written reports haven't been graded."

Cody grinned. "A-plus. Mine was an oral report. I decided to run a trial like my dad would have done."

"I'm proud of you, Cody," Mrs. Norton said. She smiled.

Cody's mother hurried into the room. "Boys!" she said. "What are you doing in here?"

"They were filling me in on the smoke bomb," Mrs. Norton said. "These things happen, I guess. Boys will be boys. Now they're going to go to the kitchen and get something to eat. Isn't there some double chocolate-fudge ice cream in the freezer?"

Cody dropped his arm from Hayden's shoulders and walked back to the kitchen, Hayden following.

"I wouldn't mind if you came over to hang out," Hayden said.

"Okay," Cody answered. "I'm here until Grandma gets better. We should make the most of it."

He looked at the kitchen clock. It wouldn't be long before Jake would be walking onstage in the club.

He'd stand in the spotlight at the mike, and he'd use Cody's joke.

Cody thought, *If I were a stand-up comic . . .*

Good evening, ladies and gentlemen. You're a fine-looking group. Of course, you can't tell much from the way people look. Take me, for instance. You might not guess that during the week, I'm a district attorney in Santa Olivia. But tonight at open-mike, I'm Cody Carter, stand-up comic, and I want to talk to you about my cousin Hayden.

You don't get to choose cousins. You have to take what you get. Having a cousin is sort of like having a brother, except you don't get a Christmas present from him, just a card. And you don't get to tell him what you really think of him, because he comes with a pair of bodyguards called an aunt and uncle. And you have a cousin forever and ever, no refunds, no returns. So I've got Hayden. Okay, he's taller than I am but he's not so tough after all. I know how to beat him at his own game. I can tell him jokes that are so funny he laughs till he cries.

About the Author

JOAN LOWERY NIXON, the grande dame of young adult mysteries, wrote more than 130 books for young readers, including *Nightmare; Nobody's There; Who Are You?; The Haunting; Murdered, My Sweet; The Trap;* and *Playing for Keeps.* She was the only four-time winner of the Edgar Allan Poe Best Young Adult Mystery Award. Her historical fiction includes the award-winning series The Orphan Train Adventures, Orphan Train Children, and Colonial Williamsburg: Young Americans.